RESERVE MY CURVES 3: THE FINALE

B.M. Hardin

I0566304

ISBN-13: 978-0692502198

ISBN-10: 069250219X

This book is a work of fiction. All persons, events, places and locales are a product of the others imagination. The story is fictitious and any thoughts of similarities are merely coincidental.

<u>Dedication</u>

This book is dedicated to a few special superstar readers, Shatisha Nash, Kendra Huskey, LaToya Denton, Earline Hamell, Terry Langston, Alnita Gray Roane, Liz Doss, and Tiffany Hudson.

Thank you all for your support and for following me on my writing journey. It is truly a blessing to have supporters like you in my corner. Thank you!

Acknowledgements

First and foremost, I want to thank my Heavenly Father for my talents and my gifts and each and every story that he has placed in me.

It is an honor and a privilege to be living my dream and walking in my purpose and for that I am forever thankful.

Also to all of my family, friends, critiques, supporters, readers and everyone else, thank you for believing in me and allowing me to share my gifts with you.

Your support truly means the world to me!

B.M. Hardin

Author B.M. Hardin's contact info:

Facebook: http://www.facbook.com/authorbm

Twitter: @BMHardin1

Instagram: @bm_hardin

Email:bmhardinbooks@gmail.com

Reserve My Curves 3: The Finale

Chapter ONE

Grant.

My sister's, Josephine's husband Grant, was the head boss at the hotel.

My first thought when I saw his name was what the--- well, you know what.

I mean how, when?

Like…what?

I remembered staring at the papers for a long while, hoping that the names on them would either change or disappear.

But they didn't.

They just didn't.

I was in so much shock, about both of them, that for a while, I'd actually stopped breathing.

I mean turning blue in the face, about to die and everything.

I just couldn't believe it.

I couldn't believe it at all.

Though the discovery about Silas being one of the bosses hurt me the most, finding out that Grant was the top boss damn near gave me a heart attack.

He was so quiet and so humble.

He hardly ever even spoke, so how in the hell could he be the ring leader of selling ass?

It just didn't make sense.

Hell, I'd never even so much as heard him curse!

Nope, I just couldn't believe it.

Something just had to be wrong.

It wasn't until I'd placed my hand on the door handle, at the police station, yesterday, that I'd decided to keep some of the papers and not turn Silas and Grant in.

Why I did it?

Hell I don't know.

I would love to give a logical reason, but I couldn't come up with one even if I tried.

Silas and Grant both deserved to go down, mainly because both of them had deceived me, but for some reason, I'd withheld all of the information pertaining to them.

The smudges of dirt on the papers that I'd kept, the ones with their names on them, told me that they were some of the papers that I'd found at Carmen's house in the vase, the day that I was shot.

They were the same papers that were hidden under all of the dirt and the ones that I'd put into my purse.

I knew Carmen had taken them.

She must have gotten them out while I was lying on the ground, shot and passed out, or on the ride to the hospital I suppose.

Knowing her, she'd been somewhere looking out of a window or something, the whole time and she'd probably seen me stash the papers in my bag from the very beginning.

I wondered why she'd taken them back to the hotel instead of taken them back to her home.

Maybe she forgot.

And I'm glad that she had.

Since the papers revealing the truth about Silas and Grant didn't exactly belong at the hotel anyway, I was sure that keeping them wouldn't raise any suspicions, since all of the other paper work was consistent.

Oh, and I couldn't forget the fact that there were already two other men in place to take the *fall* for Silas and Grant if anything happened.

Now how about that?

They had it all figured out.

On some of the paperwork it named two other men as the head bosses of the hotel.

But on the dirty papers that I still had in my possession, it had the dirty truth.

There were signed agreements that if anything ever happened, or if problems were to arise, the two men had agreed to take the fall for Silas and Grant and in return, on top of the "salary" that they had already been receiving, for years, they would get the best legal representation that money could buy, any and every string pulled that was possible and them and their families would be taken care of forever, financially, if any convictions or prison time came into play.

I couldn't believe that they'd thought so far ahead.

There was no way in the hell that I would give up my freedom for money, but there was no telling what reasons the two men had.

Hell, there's no telling what a person might do for money if they were all out of options.

I was a prime example of that.

So basically, the detective thought he had the head honchos, but really he had nothing at all, well except for the one person that he'd wanted the most…Carmen.

Carmen was behind bars and I loved it!

I was so happy about her being locked up that I wanted to jump for joy, but she wasn't the only one that deserved to be sitting in a cell.

I mean of course she knew the truth, and though she'd been arrested, I was willing to bet that she wouldn't utter a single word about Silas or Grant.

And now I guess I would be keeping the truth to myself too.

But maybe I should have thought this whole thing through just a little more.

Maybe I should have turned their asses in!

Silas had lied to me, deceived me and betrayed me.

I was no saint, but what he'd done to me just didn't make sense.

He'd known exactly who I was when he'd approached me, obviously. He'd known exactly what I was doing the entire time at the hotel and hadn't said a word.

But why?

What man in their right mind would do something like that?

How could he even want to touch me knowing that I would spend hours most days being touched by someone else?

Ooh, I was so angry at him!

And I was frustrated because I didn't have all of the answers, but I so desperately wanted them, and I'd be damned if he wasn't going to give them to me.

But how was I going to be able to believe anything that he said?

At that thought, I came back from my thoughts, to see that Silas was still standing in front of me with the papers that I had given him still in his hands.

At the sight of the dumbfounded look on his face, I started to see red.

Before I could stop myself, I smacked the spit bubbles out of his mouth, stuck my middle finger up at him and headed to the bedroom.

Bastard!

Silas stomped behind me as though he was coming to push me down or something and I almost wanted to run.

"Envy, let me explain," he growled.

I grabbed a bag and headed to the dresser.

As I opened the drawers, Silas started to talk.

"It isn't what you think."

I gave him a look that could have sent him straight to the pits of Hell, with gasoline drawers on.

How isn't it what I think?

I'd always known that it was something, something a little strange or mysterious about him, but I just couldn't put my finger on it.

But never could I have imagined that this was his big secret.

I continued to pack my bag and Silas continued to reach his hand into it and take the clothes back out of it.

"Move Silas!"

"No. You're not leaving me. I would never let you leave me, especially without you knowing the truth. It isn't what you think."

I rolled my eyes at him.

He couldn't talk himself out of this one no matter how hard he tried; this hole was way too deep.

I glanced at his other hand and noticed that he was no longer holding the papers.

What had he done with them?

Those papers were the only proof that I had, just in case I changed my mind about turning both of their lying asses in. Or at the very least the papers gave me some kind of leverage.

Why did I even give them to him in the first place?

What was I thinking?

"Envy."

Silas continued to pull the clothes out of the bag until finally I gave up and headed to the closet.

I grabbed the step stool and looked for my bag full of money on the top shelf, but it wasn't there.

What?

"Silas where the hell is my money?"

He didn't say a word.

I got down and hurriedly went to check my other two hiding spots for the other two bags of cash, but they weren't there either.

What?

What the hell is going on here?

Silas was right behind me.

"Silas where is my money? You can have the house and everything in it, just give me my money. You know the money that you allowed me to lay on my back to make without so much as saying a damn word! You make me sick. Where is my money Silas, huh?" I asked him again.

"You're not leaving me Envy," he said.

I didn't have time to play with him.

If he really thought that I was going to stay with him after finding out that he'd known about the thirteenth floor the whole time and about me, he was just as looney as everybody else had been lately.

Silas grabbed my hand and literally pulled me towards the living room.

I pushed and pulled, but he didn't let up.

He forced me to take a seat and he sat down beside me.

Why couldn't he have just been the one?

Why couldn't he have been my dream come true like I'd thought that he was?

My emotions started to take over and once I started to cry, Silas decided to speak.

"I couldn't tell you who I was Envy. How would I have looked telling you something like that? You didn't need to know. You were never even supposed to know. The business was handed over to me. I became a boss, the boss, around the same time that I'd met Carmen. To be honest, she wasn't already at the hotel when I met her, I brought her on. It's all hard to explain."

I'd stop crying to make sure that I didn't miss one word that he'd said.

I was so disappointed and angry that I thought that my head was going to explode.

I should have known that he and Carmen still had some kind of dealings.

I should have known that they were some kind of *team*.

She was his backbone in the operation, which is why she'd always thought that she had some kind of rights to him.

It explained why she gave me hell, and definitely explained why she felt like she couldn't and would never be replaced.

It all made sense.

Everything that he'd ever said to me was one big lie.

I was such a fool.

"I've been tired of the business for a long time. It was handed over to me, and I stepped down and handed it over to Grant a while ago. Grant and I are as close as brothers. His mother and my mother are actually fairly close. They'd met when my mother was in the States. They kept in touch, and my family even flew them out for vacations with us a few times. It was my idea to keep our friendship from both you and Josephine. It just made it easier," Silas said.

Huh?

What a minute, so Grant and Silas were like best friends or something?

How could that be?

They surely never acted like it around each other.

I was so confused.

"So you and Grant are best friends? This whole time y'all have known each other?"

Silas nodded.

"But why hide it?"

"It was just easier that way. Let me back up. My family actually gave the family, who owned the hotel, the money to start and open it many years ago as a favor to a white man that saved my great, great grandfather's life a long time ago. So, with my families money tied to the hotel and once the idea of the *extracurricular activities* came about, and by that I mean the thirteenth floor, there's always someone from my family in America to somewhat oversee their investment, so to speak. They got paid. We got paid. My mother had come over with my step-father, to help with hotel business many years ago. She'd met Grant's mother and my mother raved of how close their friendship was, and how much she loved her cooking. Some issues came up and my *parents* headed back to Africa and someone else was sent in their place. But she never forgot about Grant's family. And she made sure that they didn't forget about her. They spent many of summers with us and I'd even come to stay with them here for a summer or two. Our families are very close, which is why they didn't have a problem with letting me hand the top position over to Grant."

Silas had always been fairly private about his family. He didn't speak of them much, and when he did, it was always short and simple.

He led me to believe that he had been cut off and that they despised him, but listening to him now, I was sure that he had just used that as a part of his sad ass cover up.

"I loved to be here in America. A life of royalty was fine. But I wanted a little more freedom than that life allowed. When it was time for me to be groomed to take over at the hotel, I did it with no hesitation. Of course I'd told Grant a long time ago the truth about the hotel, and he'd begged to get in on it, for the money, for his family. Your sister actually seen me a few times, years ago, but she didn't seem to remember me. I think she'd thought that I was one of Silas's co-workers when he had a real job. I thought it was best to keep my distance from his family."

I let out a deep breath.

I had my lies, my secrets, and my flaws, but damn!

And he wasn't even done telling me the whole story yet.

"I'd played my part as the top dog for a few years, and Grant helped with finances. And after a while, I'd wanted out. I craved a normal life. So I handed it over to Grant. Grant is the top dog in charge. Or should I say was? Grant loved the power and the money. I taught him everything that I knew. I stayed around to oversee, though he had it down pact. It was just a matter of timing. Soon I was cutting all ties. To be honest, had we not became an item, I would've been gone over a year ago, but since you were already on board, I was just waiting on you. I felt better about being in the mix while you were still there. Strange but true. You could have quit at any time, and I would have made sure that you were fine, but you never took my advice. I would've handled the contract and Carmen."

Oh now you tell me!

I just didn't know what to say so I didn't say anything.

Silas was stupid and so was Grant.

I mean, they acted like complete strangers in the beginning!

I mean, yes, they were cordial now, and talked about guy stuff here and there when they were around each other, but they didn't act like the best buds that they actually were.

Pitiful! Just down right ridiculous!

It was all just stupid, and I didn't know which one of them I wanted to stab the most.

I'd known Grant since he and Josephine was all of seventeen years old. He was Josephine's second guy friend, and right after their high school graduation, they got married.

He'd always been the same; hardworking, kind, quiet and passive.

He'd surely never mentioned an African friend or second-like family.

And if he had, Josephine had managed to leave that out of our conversations.

I'd always thought that he had a regular job.

He was always professionally dressed and he had always taken good care of Josephine and the kids.

He just seemed regular. A regular ole' *average Joe*.

But the truth was that he was just damn good at pretending.

Unbelievable!

And I was telling on his ass too!

I surely was.

My sister deserved to know the truth about the man that she called her husband…right?

But they were doing so good.

She was finally being faithful to him and they were about to renew their wedding vows.

I couldn't mess all of that up could I?

Those thoughts had been part of the reason that I'd kept the papers from the detective in the first place.

I'd already loss two of my sisters, no matter how you looked at it, and I didn't want to lose the only one that I had left.

If she felt like I ruined her marriage, or took her husband away from her in a sense, I was sure that Josephine would never forgive me.

So, what was I going to do?

And getting back to Silas, here he was telling me all of this, yet saying that he didn't want me to leave him.

The nerve of him!

I'm sorry, but if knowing that I was lying down with random men for money four days a week, wasn't enough to make him showcase his love for me by putting a stop to it, I had to reevaluate if what he felt for me was love at all.

Why would any man accept that?

Something still just wasn't right.

"I'd seen you a time or two, downstairs, at the hotel before approaching you that day at the café. And then one day, I saw your information and photo added to the thirteenth floor database and I found myself staring at you for what seemed like hours. And then that day you showed up at the outside café, I figured that maybe I could get to know you. At first I wasn't going to say anything, but I just couldn't help myself. I just had to have you," Silas admitted.

I smacked him again as the last words came out of his mouth and I could tell that this time, he wanted to hit my ass back.

He balled up his fists, but after staring at me for a minute or so, he relaxed.

He should have just left me the hell alone!

I was doing just fine.

I was lonely, but I was fine.

"So all of this, everything between us was a lie?" I just had to ask.

"No. My love for you is real. It was just a bad situation."

Tell me about it.

At this point, I didn't believe anything that Silas had ever said to me.

Everything that had ever come out of his mouth was suspect.

Maybe he was telling me the whole story now, since the hotel operation had been shut down, but I wasn't even sure if I could trust or believe everything he'd just said.

So, now I had to figure out my next move.

Horizon was with Josephine, so I figured that I could get a few of our things together and head back to my old house; parent's house.

I was so thankful that I hadn't decided to get rid of it. Now all I needed was my money.

What in the hell had Silas done with it?

And why had he moved it in the first place?

And how did he know about the other two hiding places?

Nosey ass.

"Silas, where is my money?"

"You're not leaving me Envy."

"Yes I am. What are you going to do? Make me stay?"

"If I have to."

What?

He couldn't make me do a damn thing that I didn't want to do.

I stood to my feet and Silas stood as well.

I damn near ran back to our bedroom and started to tear it apart looking for my bags of cash again.

I had hardly ever touched it, so I couldn't even begin to estimate how much it was.

I was always spending Silas's money, or if I needed small things, I would spend the small check that I got from the hotel as though I was still a *regular* maid.

"Silas give me my damn money!"

"It's gone."

I looked at him as though he was stupid.

Gone?

Where the hell did it go?

"Silas, I'm not playing with you. Where is it?"

"It's in a safe place. You can have it back after the wedding."

What?

Wedding?

There wasn't going to be a damn wedding!

Our entire relationship had been built on nothing but lies.

His lies, my lies, everybody's lies and he still thought that I was going to marry him?

Yeah right!

"I can't believe that marriage is still on your mind. At this point, I can't see myself marrying you Silas, like ever. Not after all this. And how did you even know to take my money and hide it or whatever you did with it anyway?"

"Carmen told me what you did."

Well of course she did.

She must have told him once she'd discovered that I'd stolen the paperwork.

Being that Silas was one of the bosses that explained why she hadn't come to my house to cause a scene.

But why would she give him a heads up?

She was going down and he was going to get away, since he and Grant had someone to pay the time for their crimes, so why was she so damn dedicated to him?

"So, she gave you a sort of head's up?"

"Of course she did."

"Why Silas?"

"Why not Envy?"

"So after the divorce and the affair that you'd had with her sister, her own flesh and blood, she still has some kind of feelings for you? And furthermore, after all of that, she still wanted to work for you at the hotel? And you allowed her to? Why? What's the real story with you two?"

"Business is business. She did her job well and she wanted to continue doing it, so I let her stay. It didn't bother me none. Carmen owes me her life and so I know in return she'll always be loyal."

What the hell was that supposed to mean?

How did she owe him her life?

What because of the money?

No, I was sure that wasn't it.

"You and Carmen have had something going on this whole time haven't you?"

"What? Hell no. Carmen is *sick*."

Oh yes, that's right, Carmen had HIV.

Immediately I looked at Silas suspiciously.

"Who did she get the HIV from Silas huh?"

He looked at me as though he was surprised that I actually knew the piece of information.

He looked at me as though he'd wanted to tell me that it was none of my damn business, but he knew better than to say that.

"I don't know Envy. Her personal life isn't my business. I can remember her telling me about a bad date or two, but she and I have never talked about anything more. We mostly talked about business. I only know about the HIV because the news of it damn near drove her crazy; well, it made her even crazier than she already was. After the news, Carmen was never the same. She'd always been a little *off*, well not just a little. But she turned into someone else. Someone vicious. She'd always been mean but she turned pure evil."

I'd stopped looking and sat on the edge of the bed as I listened to Silas.

He went on to explain more about the real relationship between he and Carmen and he'd also said something very interesting.

He'd told me the truth about the start of their relationship.

He'd told me that initially, he'd met Nicole, his deceased wife and Carmen's dead sister.

He'd said that Carmen's sister was an employee at the bank that he'd used back then and they'd always been a little flirty with each other.

But on the visit that he'd finally told himself that he was going to ask her on a date, he learned that she'd recently quit and was gone.

A few months later, he ran into Carmen and almost confused the two. He'd initially approached her because she reminded him of Nicole, but he said that Carmen had a little something extra.

He said he loved her brains and her beauty and he said that they started to date, and soon ended up getting married.

He'd said that Carmen had lied and told him that her whole family was dead, but one day, after they were already married, they ran into Nicole, and they identified each other as sisters.

Silas said immediately he'd recognized her but he was already in love with Carmen and for the most part, it was too late.

Nothing was ever mentioned and all was well.

Silas said that he and Carmen were happily married for a while, but he said that it didn't last long.

Carmen and her ways became unbearable and he found out a few of her secrets.

The truth about Carmen was scary.

She'd not only killed her father, as she'd told me, oh no, she'd left out most of the story.

Carmen had killed her whole family, except for Nicole because she was actually the youngest and a baby at the time.

She'd stabbed her father, mother and her other siblings, repeatedly, while they slept.

According to what Silas had found out about her, she'd been hospitalized several times for severe anger issues, paranoia, and even depression at such a young age, before the incident even occurred.

There were suspicions of foul play and of abuse; both verbal and maybe even sexual but not from her father as Carmen had said…but from her mother.

The records showed that every time Carmen had to be hospitalized, after a few days, her mother always came and got her, and from observations it appeared that Carmen was terrified of her, but that the mother had some kind of obsession with Carmen.

She wouldn't even let her get the help that she needed from wanting Carmen in her space.

And then one night, in Carmen's early teens, she killed them all, except for the baby that was sleeping in the crib beside her parents bed.

She'd gotten off with insanity and mental illness and served years institutionalized.

She'd only been released a year or two before meeting Silas.

Silas said he knew something was wrong with her after he caught her screaming and threatening her reflection one morning in their bathroom mirror, so he went digging, and paid a few people, who paid someone else, and that's what he came up with.

Silas explained that he found it amazing with how good she was with business affairs and logistics considering that she wasn't always in her right mind, but he said that Carmen was darn near a genius.

He called her the smartest person he'd ever known.

He'd offered to get her more help once she started acting out and became worse, but she refused and he'd said that he'd given her an ultimatum.

If she didn't allow him to get her the best treatment and hospitalization that money could buy, he would divorce her.

Long story short, she really thought that she didn't need help, and he divorced her without thinking twice about it.

He'd said that he'd kept Carmen's truth from Nicole, being that she had no idea what Carmen had really done.

She'd always been told that her family had been murdered, but not by her sister. They'd told her that she hadn't been touched and that Carmen only survived because she had been in the hospital at the time.

She said that she never bothered to try to find the truth and that she'd only wanted to know where Carmen was.

She always kept some kind of communication with Carmen once she was old enough, and before the issue with Silas and Nicole, Silas said that Nicole was probably the only person that Carmen had ever truly cared about.

He'd said that he and Nicole still just happened and he still said that he didn't regret anything that they'd shared.

He'd really felt as though it was true love.

I was speechless, confused, appalled, and everything else in between.

This was the worst relationship experience…ever!

"Carmen knew you were up to something for a while. She didn't know what, but we were prepared. I was the one that really got the papers out of your purse," Silas said.

What?

I asked him that and he'd said no…old lying bastard!

"I gave them to Carmen and she was supposed to take them back home, but I'm starting to think that she took them back to the hotel on purpose. She wanted to get caught. She and I were both tired. And with all of Carmen's issues, psychological issues, hospitalization history and more, I'm sure that she probably won't even stand trial. At the most she might be sentenced to be institutionalized, again, but even they wouldn't keep her this time. Carmen pays the entire board of the local mental hospital, faithfully, just in case she was ever sentenced to go back there again."

Damn.

These folks were just paying folks for everything!

They thought that their money made them above the law and above all of the rules.

And apparently it did.

Carmen knew what she was doing.

She'd expressed to me numerous of times about being tired of the hotel so I believed Silas on that and I wouldn't doubt that Carmen wanted to get caught, just to get out.

And thinking about her smiling as she was being led to the police car in handcuffs and winking at me as they drove away, I was sure that she was positive that she was going to walk away from it all; which meant that she was still going to be a problem.

But she was Silas's problem, not mine.

I was done with this.

Silas had said more than enough and I knew that there was nothing left for me and him to discuss.

"Silas, just give me my money so I can go."

He didn't move or say a word.

"Carmen told you that something was about to go down and you take my money to try and use it to make me stay?"

"Trust me, you won't be going anywhere," Silas said.

Oh really?

Well I could show him better than I could tell him.

I walked out of the room and headed to the living room.

I grabbed my purse and my keys and headed out of the door.

I locked the doors once inside of the car as I watched Silas head in my direction.

Putting the car in reverse, I backed out of the driveway. From the street, I glanced back at Silas who was now on his cell phone, as I drove away.

My mind was racing and my heart was pounding.

I tried to remember everything that he'd said but I just couldn't get my thoughts together.

Silas and Carmen were both like a bad dream.

The drama surrounding them just never seemed to cease and I was right in the middle of it.

With everything that Silas had revealed, I'd definitely made the wrong choice by going back to the hotel.

I shouldn't have turned back.

No matter how desperate I was, I shouldn't have gone back.

And Silas had given me so many signs that something wasn't right with him, but I hadn't taken them or my way out.

I hadn't taken them for what they were and got away from him like I should have a long time ago.

No I couldn't change the past.

But I could change the present and the future.

And I wanted Silas and Carmen out of my life…for good!

He was like a Devil with a big ass bank account and I didn't know what to call Carmen.

She'd killed almost her whole family?

She'd been institutionalized?

And she'd been sexually taken advantage of…maybe?

And on top of all of that, she was sick, and from the sound of it all maybe it wasn't by consensual relations?

And I thought that I had it bad!

I'd known that something was really wrong with Carmen all along, and I'd been right.

But she had some serious issues and though I couldn't stand her, learning all of that, I kind of could see how she could be just a little messed up.

Genuinely, I hoped that somehow, someone made her get the help that she so desperately needed.

And she really, really needed it.

But according to Silas, she'd pretty much paid everybody in charge of the mental hospital to make sure that she didn't get any better, at least not at that one she wouldn't.

Maybe she liked being psycho.

Maybe Silas and the hotel made her worse.

Maybe getting away from it all she would help her get better.

I don't know, but one thing I did know was that Detective Wiley is going to have a damn fit if, or more like when she walks.

This entire bust would have basically been for nothing.

Sure he got the credit for a major take-down, but Carmen was what he'd wanted most, his whole point of going after the hotel in the first place. And I had a feeling that he still wasn't going to get what he wanted.

I'd warned him that he couldn't be sure of the type of power, money, and people in connection with Carmen, but I was sure that he was about to find out.

Entering the highway, I had about an hour or so to get back to my old house, so that left me with plenty of time to think.

Silas had all of my money.

My bank account didn't have hardly anything in it but a few hundred dollars, so I needed my money.

He couldn't keep it.

He had no right to touch anything that was mine.

He must've searched for the other two bags while I was at the police station the day before, or while I was watching the hotel bust.

I wondered what Carmen had said to him about me taking the papers from her office.

Had I been thinking, I would have taken the money out of the house that same night, after discovering that Silas was a boss, but I hadn't.

I was too busy debating as to whether or not I was going to confront Silas or if it was in my best interest to pretend as though I didn't know.

Thinking of it, my behavior probably gave it away too. I was salty as hell and trying to bite my tongue while being in his presence had me as hot as hen's piss.

I knew that I wasn't going to be able to keep it to myself, but I figured that it was probably better to wait until the bust had taken place before I opened my mouth.

Unfortunately, Silas still had the papers, so I guess there goes my evidence if I ever changed my mind.

But it was what it was.

I just wanted my money and my life back.

As Silas had stated, I too just wanted to be normal.

A normal life would do just fine.

While I drove, I couldn't help but think about Grant too.

It's always the quiet ones that you had to watch out for.

Never would I have guessed that he would even want to be involved in something that involved sex and other women.

I swear it just didn't seem like him at all.

And now what was I supposed to do about it?

How could I keep something like this from Josephine?

But how could I tell her something that would surely mess up her marriage?

I was sure that she would flip all the way out, but was telling her really necessary?

Was it really worth it?

Hell, it wasn't like he was going to still be running the thirteenth floor, or even going to jail for it, so maybe mentioning it would be a bad idea.

Maybe it was pointless.

Whoo! I was giving myself a headache!

It was just so much to deal with all at once.

But there was a tad bit of good in the midst of all of this.

I was done with the hotel.

And I'd avoided going to jail.

Not to mention that Carmen was behind bars, at least for now.

So, I did have a few things to be grateful for.

Now, I just needed my money and I needed to get missing.

My phone rung over and over with calls from Silas but I refused to answer them.

There was just no way I was going to be with him.

He was a fool to even suggest that we try to make things work and on top of that, he still wanted to get married.

What the hell was he smoking?

Silas was delusional and he had better find a genie and three wishes if he thought for a second that he would see me in a white dress, walking down aisle toward him to music, holding flowers and all that other bull crap.

It just wasn't going to happen.

Not now and not ever!

I ignored his calls over and over again and before I could even turn onto the street of my parent's house, I could see the smoke.

And then I saw the flames.

My house, the house that had belonged to my parents, was up in flames…again.

But this time, the house was burning down.

It was pretty much gone as though it had been burning for a long while.

And get this, fire fighters were there…but they weren't doing anything.

They were just standing there, chatting, as though a fire wasn't taking place right in front of them.

I didn't see even one water hose spraying water on the house to control the flame.

I didn't see anybody running around in a panic trying to make sure that no one was in there or trying to figure out want to do next.

Everybody was just standing there.

Everybody was calm.

What the hell is wrong with this picture?

I jumped out of the car and immediately started to ask questions.

No one seemed to know how the fire had started, but they assured me that the house couldn't be saved.

It was gone.

The house that my parents had raised us in and worked hard for, and that I had laid on my back to pay back off, was burning down to the ground right in front of me.

I thought about all of the things that were now lost like pictures and things left behind to remember the people that I'd loved the most.

My life absolutely, positively, sucked!

Everything was always going wrong.

After a few minutes the head fireman in charge, I suppose, walked over to me and reached me his phone.

I looked at him confused as he continued to reach it out towards me.

Finally, I took it and placed it on my ear.

"Hello? Envy. So when will you be back home?" Silas asked.

What?

What was he doing on the fireman's phone?

Ugh, they had connections everywhere!

I'd left my phone in the car, so I'm guessing he'd called the man to see if I'd arrived.

"Silas, did you do this?"

He was quiet.

"Not technically. I might have made a small call," he said.

My mouth opened wide, and the next thing I knew, I was hollering, screaming and cursing so bad that even the grown folks started to cover their ears.

And just before throwing the fireman's phone to the ground, and stomping on it, I heard Silas say.

"Okay Envy, I'll see you when you get home."

Damn lunatic!

****

Chapter TWO

"Envy, you don't have any money, come home," Silas said.

Can you believe that I'd gone to the bank to get whatever little cash that I had in there out, just for them to tell me that the account was empty and had been closed due to some bogus ass sixty day old overdraft?

Get the hell out of here!

Yet, I'd just deposited a small *regular* maid's check the week before, not to mention that I'd recently used my bank card for gas, but no matter who I talked to, they all tried to tell me the same thing which could only mean one thing.

Silas was behind it all.

I was sure that he had something to do with it.

He wasn't God for crying out loud!

Why was it that he could do things that he wasn't supposed to be able to do?

I couldn't help but wonder how he and his family, or whoever had gotten so many different American ties, and it only made me even more afraid of whom the real Silas actually was.

So basically, I was broke and eventually I was going to have to do something about it.

I'd thought to ask Josephine for a few dollars, but she was only going to ask questions and I wasn't sure of what answers to give her just yet.

I was just glad that Horizon was with her so that I could really try to figure some things out.

I was sure that Grant knew that I knew about him and his previous role at the hotel by now, and I was sure that he was on pins and needles, waiting for my next move.

But for now, he was in the clear, but I didn't know for how long.

I had to get myself together first before I started messing up my sister's relationship.

Since I didn't have any money, thanks to Silas, I'd slept in the car overnight, in the driveway of my burnt down home.

I couldn't believe that Silas would have gone that far, but it just showed me that I didn't know him at all.

It showed me just how ruthless he really was.

And it also showed me just how far he was willing to get to get what he wanted.

I'd only eaten a candy bar, so I knew that I had to do something quick because my stomach was definitely on empty.

And on top of that, it was cold.

Silas would always tell me to keep cash in my purse, but I never did.

I never listened.

And now I was paying for it.

I was furious at him for what he'd done to my house; well, more like what he'd had someone else do to it, but of course he was the one to blame.

I wasn't sure of what I was going to do to him when I saw him again, but he had better believed that he'd just caused a war.

I couldn't believe that he was doing all of this to make sure that I didn't have anywhere else to go.

And the sad thing was that he was succeeding.

He was messing with my money. He was messing with everything.

And I was willing to bet that he wasn't going to stop until he got what he wanted.

At this point, I didn't have a choice but to go home to him.

I was cold, I was hungry, and I hadn't washed my ass in over twenty-four hours, so *Ms. Pussy* definitely had one hell of an attitude.

He'd left me no choice.

I arrived to see Silas sitting on the front porch as though he was expecting me.

Why won't he just go away and leave me alone?

He couldn't possibly really love me after all of the lies that he'd told me. But then again, no one loves exactly the same.

And at the same time, I'd been lying to him too, and no one could tell me that I hadn't loved him, because I had.

Or maybe in a way I still do.

I was confused.

But *we* could never work.

He couldn't have loved me and allowed me to be a whore all at the same time.

He just couldn't have.

Whatever it was just couldn't be love.

I wasn't sure what it was, but it wasn't love.

Not the kind of love that I wanted for that matter.

So, why was he fighting for something that we never really had in the first place?

Our relationship was doomed from the very beginning.

And the fact that he was trying to leave me broke and without a home if I didn't want to be with him, just confirmed that he cared more about himself than he cared about me.

I guess I took too long to get out of the car because after a while, Silas got up and walked over to the car.

He waited for me to roll down the window.

"Envy, let's talk."

"We already talked Silas."

He seemed as though he was becoming frustrated.

"Well, let's talk again. Let's start over."

I shook my head no.

"Yes."

"No."

"Well if you leave, where are you going to go? What are you going to do? You don't have any money. I just got word that they are officially shutting the hotel down for good. You can't go back as a maid. So what are you going to do?"

I hadn't watched the news yet but I'd heard a good bit about what was being speculated about the hotel on the radio.

I'd known from the start that shutting its doors was inevitable.

"I'll figure it out."

Silas took a deep breath.

I could tell that he was really getting upset like he had the right to be.

But there was no way in hell that I could stay with him after all that had gone on.

"Envy, let's go in the house and talk."

I shook my head no again.

I guess that was the last straw because before I had a chance to blink, Silas opened my driver's side door, and pulled me out of the car by my hair.

And I mean he was literally pulling me, head and hair first out of the car.

Really?

I was in shock at first and it was as though I was having a bad dream or something.

I couldn't believe it.

But when reality kicked in, I started screaming for help and throwing punches his way all at the same time.

"Hey Silas, how are you doing over there buddy?" our next door neighbor said, stepping outside at the sound of all the noise.

Silas was still pulling me by my hair towards the front door and I was still screaming.

"Everything is going just fine." Silas responded and with his words, the man from next door said okay and went back inside of his house.

What?

Wait a minute…what!

He'd gone in as though he hadn't seen a thing.

Silas opened the front door and damn near threw me inside.

As soon as I was loose, I attacked him but he picked me up and carried me to the bedroom.

He threw me on the bed and then closed the bedroom door and sat in front of it.

I started to throw stuff at him but he only smacked it away.

"How dare you! You said you would never put your hands on me!" I screamed.

"And I haven't. You just needed a little help coming inside."

Who was this man?

This wasn't *my* Silas.

I felt as though I didn't know him at all.

Hell in all reality, I didn't.

Everything I thought I knew about him was what he'd wanted me to believe and most of it was a lie.

I screamed and fussed.

And fussed and screamed some more.

But Silas didn't say anything.

His phone ranged and I made as much noise as possible and shouted out that he was keeping me against my will and that I needed help.

Silas hung up, and continued to just sit there.

For starters, he was being too damn calm about everything, the whole time, which gave me the feeling that he was even more dangerous than I realized.

"Silas just leave me alone. Just let me go. I need my money so I can just go."

"Give me a chance. Let's work on us until the wedding date. If it doesn't work out by then, then I will let you go. It's only a few months away. Let's just see what happens from now until then."

I wanted to call him so many names that I couldn't get them out of my mouth fast enough.

He can't make me do anything.

I'm a grown ass woman!

And then he said that he will *let* me go.

He won't *let* me do a damn thing!

"No Silas, no," I said to him harshly.

"Why? Thanks to you, there's no more hotel business, no more thirteenth floor, no more *reserving your curves*. We have a clean slate. A fresh start. We can really try to work it out. I love you, Envy. You might not think so but I really do. And I can't live without you or Horizon."

At the mention of her name, I thought about my daughter.

I thought about how much I loved her and I thought about how much she loved him.

He was the only father figure that she'd ever known and she adored Silas.

But she would get over it.

And then again…what was I really going to do?

I didn't have any money, not within my reach, and I didn't have a home to go back to.

And Silas wasn't going to give me the money back, unless I did what he said.

I was sure of it.

So, that meant that I had to find a job, and I already knew how hard that was going to be for me.

So what was I supposed to do now?

But I just couldn't stay here.

I just couldn't stay with Silas.

I didn't trust him any further than I could see him and I didn't know what he was really capable of.

I just wanted out.

"Silas, just please give me my money and let me go."

He looked at me as though he wanted to choke the life out of me or as if he was upset that he couldn't change my mind with his words, no matter what he said.

"You *will* give us a chance. Or you will go to jail and I will take Horizon."

Excuse me?

What the hell was he talking about?

I was in the clear when it came to the charges with the hotel, so what did he mean?

And taking my daughter…over my dead body!

"Silas, what are you talking about? And you're not taking my daughter anywhere."

Though we'd already handled the adoption process, and everything was signed, his lawyer was holding on to the paperwork until the day after the wedding.

We'd finally fully agreed that it was just better to do it once we were husband and wife.

But then it hit me.

What if Silas had already had the papers turned in?

He'd been the one to get everything going for the process, so who's to say that he didn't have all of them in his back pocket too?

Not to mention that my signature was already on everything.

Oh hell no!

"You heard what I said."

"No, Silas explain," I replied to him.

Silas stood to his feet and came over to me.

His face had softened but I knew that he was up to no good.

"You remember that *hit* you ordered years ago?"

Hit?

What was he talking about?

I didn't order any kind of hit.

Wait a minute.

Oh…no…wait.

He couldn't possibly know about that.

Could he?

I thought about Josephine and the guy that she'd been with before Grant.

She was only about sixteen but he was in college and in that whole "I can screw any woman I want" stage.

I was very overprotective in those days and I'd tried to get him to back off and leave Josephine alone but he refused and that's when I'd gotten Keymar's drug dealing brother to follow him and shoot him down one day as he was getting into his car.

He'd looked at me like a sister, and he hadn't mind doing it.

He'd owed me a small favor anyway.

It was a horrible thing to do, and I wasn't proud of it but I couldn't let him hurt my sister.

I would do anything for my family.

I'd always been that way.

It was a careless decision and just something that happened.

Josephine had taken it pretty hard, since she'd been caught up in that whole first boyfriend, first love, nonsense, but only months later she met Grant.

And they've been together ever since.

But how did Silas know about that secret?

Keymar's brother had been in prison for years on drug charges.

He and his gang were never caught on the murder, but he'd gotten so many years behind living the fast life and making fast money.

"I can tell you are thinking about it so I'll confirm it. Yes, I have a signed confession that you ordered him to kill and he's willing to say that it was a paid hit. The police would have a field day with information on a case that was never solved and years old. When we first started dating, I spent the necessary resources to find out everything that I could about you. Everybody has secrets. You just have to be willing to find them. He's the brother of Horizon's father and after just one visit and putting enough money on his books to last him a lifetime, he told me about what he'd done for you. But your secret is safe with me...if you just give us one more chance."

He was going to blackmail me to be with him?

Really?

I felt as though I was about to die.

I couldn't believe Keymar's brother had told and I definitely couldn't believe *inspector* Silas.

What is wrong with folks with money?

Just because you have money, power and resources, that doesn't mean that you go messing around in people's lives and in their past.

Who does that?

And now he was trying to use it against me?

He was trying to make me stay in a relationship with him or send me to jail and take my child away from me?

Who in the hell does he think that he is!

"Just give us one more chance. I know I'm not who you thought that I was and of course I knew exactly who you were all along, but I love you anyway. Now I want you to learn to love me, the real me."

This man just wasn't going to quit.

He was crazy!

Like, I was just at a loss for words.

And I knew that this fool was going to do just what he'd said that he would do if I didn't comply.

"Silas, it's just a lot. I mean you were one of the bosses at the hotel, and all of the truths about you, your past and Carmen. I just don't see how we can get past it all. I don't know why you would even want to. I'm no angel, but of course you know that already. There's just no way that you could possibly think that we could have a future," I said to him.

Internally, I was as hot as Hell's fire.

I was so angry that even if I tried, I wouldn't be able to express it.

But I was trying to play at the strings of his heart.

You catch more bees with honey, so if I wanted results, my type of results from Silas, I was going to have to soften and sweeten up.

"That's just it though Envy. I don't have to lie about it or hide it anymore. And neither do you. We can finally have the life that we always wanted. I have more money than you could possibly imagine. I don't have to worry about the police coming for me. I have resources and connections all over the world. We would be just fine. I can have any woman I want Envy, but I only want you. Just you Envy and a life with you and Horizon. I'm tired. Let's just try. All I'm asking is that we try."

Silas touched my hand and I flinched.

I didn't know what to think as I stared at him.

He looked sincere but he was a man of so much power, and of so many secrets, that I was damn near scared to be in the same room with him.

And I definitely hadn't forgotten about him dragging me into the house by my hair.

Hell no I hadn't forgotten about it at all!

I'd always known that he'd had some of those *slap a bitch* qualities.

But for me, his actions only confirmed that he still had other sides to him that I had yet to see, and that I didn't want to.

But here he was, asking me, begging me, blackmailing me for another chance at love.

He'd said it himself, and I was positive that it was true that he could have any woman that he wanted.

He was attractive.

He was rich.

So I was sure that he could.

He could start fresh and she wouldn't know about his past or the hotel and they would be just fine.

So why me?

Why did he still want me?

I just didn't understand.

As we sat in silence, I started to think about the situation a little more in depth and in a different direction.

I mean, was it really all that bad?

Yes, he'd lied about being one of the bosses of the thirteenth floor, and in my opinion, if he really loved me like he claimed to, there was no way in hell that he would have been okay with other men touching me.

I mean most men would at the least be jealous or wanting the head of the man that touched or even looked at their woman in the wrong way.

But not Silas.

But then again, he was trying to hide his identity and keep his position a secret, so maybe he just dealt with it the best way that he could when no one was watching.

I mean even I knew that sometimes you had to go to extreme measures to make sure that the truth stayed hidden, to make sure a secret stayed untold and to make sure that a few skeletons stayed buried.

And to think about it, he was always pressuring me to quit, so I'm certain if I had he would have made sure that nothing would have happened to me.

Hell, he was one of the bosses, so I was certain that if anybody could have gotten me out of my contract, he could.

Even though Carmen had tried to give me a little jail scare that one time.

I wondered if Silas knew about that.

Still yet, the entire time, he'd begged me to quit.

He knew that he could have made the contract disappear.

But why couldn't he just have said that?

This entire situation was just silly!

And also a little frightening, worrisome, and pathetic. But silly to say the least.

And it would be even crazier to try to work it all out…right?

But it was all over as he'd said.

The hotel was gone, Carmen was gone, at least for now, and basically we could start over.

We could start brand new and neither one of us had to lie about the hotel anymore.

I was so confused by the situation, but at the end of the day, everything that I'd ever done was in hopes of having a better life for myself and for my daughter.

That's all I'd truly ever wanted.

Everything I had ever done had been for my family.

Every wrong decision had been for the love of my loved ones.

The *hit* as Silas had called, it was to protect Josephine.

The cry wolf incident when I was younger was to protect Tia.

And taking the position on the thirteenth floor had only been so that I could provide for my child and my pregnant sister at the time, who had only ended up in the situation, end later on dead, from trying to help me.

I'd helped the detective to avoid jail, and now that Silas was threating to send me there anyway, I just couldn't let that happen.

I looked at him.

To be honest, though I wanted to hate him, I didn't.

No matter how angry I was at him, I still loved him.

He'd shown me so much kindness and it was hard for me to accept the possibility that all of it was just for show.

Someway, somehow, his love if that's what he wanted to call it, just had to be real.

We both just sat there, for hours and said nothing.

After all, what was I supposed to say?

"I guess I'll bring her home a day or two before Christmas. Or since we are coming down for the holiday, how about I just bring her home on that day," Josephine said.

It was late December and it was a lot colder outside than usual.

But it was even colder in my house and in my bed.

I was still on the fence with everything concerning Silas and I, but I was still in the house.

I didn't really have anywhere else to go.

We didn't talk much.

It was almost as though he was just fine with the fact that I was just still in his space.

"Okay. Josephine, can I ask you something?" I asked my sister.

I still didn't know if I was going to tell her the truth about her husband Grant or not.

Who was I to mess up her marriage?

He'd been living a lie, and I was sure that Josephine wouldn't approve of what he had been doing, but the thirteenth floor was history.

So, was this another secret that I should just take to my grave?

Maybe.

"What does Grant do for a living? I know you've always said that he was busy and worked long hours. I'd always seen him in suits, so I imagine that it's something on the professional side," I said to her.

"Girl no, he's a pimp."

My mouth became extremely dry and I couldn't get my words out fast enough.

So she knew?

I mean, no, he wasn't exactly a pimp, but that was definitely one way of putting it.

"What?"

"Well not a pimp. He used to be an accountant but he was fired a few years ago. Then he ended up involved in this whole illegal business where rich men paid for sex. From what he'd said he dealt with the finances. He didn't get his hands dirty. He'd said that someone had offered him to come on as a partner and he took the position. To be honest, I never questioned him much on it because I was hoping that he'd gotten tied up in whatever it was that he was involved in and had either gotten killed or went to prison, you know since I was having an affair with Mark and all. But here lately, since we plan to make it work, I'd started to worry about him and just as I was going to bring up the topic, boom, he told me a few days ago that the job was over. He also told me that he'd made a lot more money than I'd thought that he had and that he wanted to start living, spending and enjoying it, and maybe even relocate. But I don't want to go too far from you. We're all that we have left," Josephine closed her statement.

I was flabbergasted.

Grant had told her the truth?

Really?

Well, I mean not exactly the whole truth but he'd actually put her in the loop.

Wow. Now that's how you do it.

That's what you call love.

I couldn't believe that Josephine hadn't saw a problem with it but as she'd said, she had been so busy screwing our sister Sonni's husband that she hadn't cared that her own husband was selling women's asses to the highest bidder.

I found it remarkable that he actually trusted Josephine with majority of the information.

He must really love and trust her.

See, that's what love is.

He knew that she could have ruined him, but he didn't care because he truly loved and trusted her.

Silas hadn't given me the same courtesy, but then again, our situation was completely different.

But still.

Even though he hadn't been one hundred percent honest with her, I sure as hell wasn't going to break the news to her.

She was happy now.

They were in such a good place.

Grant was free from all of the hotel business so really, there wasn't a point in running off with my mouth.

She knew enough.

She knew what she needed to know.

Now, I needed to worry about me.

Josephine and I chatted a little while longer and I hung up the phone.

Throwing the phone on the bed, I turned around to find that Silas was just standing there.

I clutched my chest.

He'd scared the crap out of me!

He was just standing there, looking at me, holding flowers.

I hadn't even heard him come into the room.

"Silas, you scared me."

"Sorry. And if you had asked, I could have told you that Josephine knew about Grant. He'd told her enough," Silas said as he reached me the flowers.

Unfortunately, I agreed.

I simply nodded and smelled the flowers.

"Thank you."

Silas nodded and came closer to me.

He touched me and my juices began to flow without my permission.

Despite what I was feeling, *she* wanted him terribly.

But sex was the last thing on my mind.

Kind of.

"Hold on," Silas said and walked out of the bedroom and closed the door.

Suddenly, he started to knock.

"Silas what are you knocking for?"

He didn't answer me, he just continued to knock.

"Um, come in, I guess."

Silas opened the bedroom door and walked over to me.

"Hello, I'm Silas," he said and reached out his hand.

I looked at him strangely.

What is he up to now?

"Let's start over. Completely over. Hello, my name is Silas," he said again.

I couldn't help but grin.

He always had that side to him that tried so hard to please me, I just hated that the bad outweighed the good.

Or did it?

Did the bad outweigh the good?

I really couldn't answer that question.

But for the moment, I guess going along with him was the appropriate thing to do.

"I'm Envy."

"Nice to meet you Envy. Let me tell you about myself. I was married, divorced. Then I married again, but my wife and daughter both died. My family is African royalty. I come from money and I have more than enough of it. Basically, I inherited the family business. It was an illegal business involving money, sex and women. I was the head of the operation, but recently passed it on. But the business was finally brought down, so now, I'm just a man looking for happily ever after, and I was hoping that I could find it with you," Silas said and though I didn't want to…

I smiled.

***

"Merry Christmas!" Josephine chimed as Horizon leaped into my arms.

She was growing like a weed and I couldn't believe that she was going to be going to school soon.

It just blew my mind how fast the time had gone.

She kissed my cheek and then ran towards Silas.

"Daddy! Daddy! Daddy!" Horizon screamed until she was in Silas's arms and heading towards the Christmas tree.

I'd noticed that she'd started to refer to him as her father a little while ago.

I didn't bother to correct her because after all, I was planning to be his wife and he was going to be the only Daddy that she ever knew or had.

And he was going to be adopting her.

But now I wasn't so sure.

"You look good," Josephine said as she hugged me.

She looked good too, just as she had been lately.

But this look was different.

This look had big money written all over it.

Grant must have really loosened the reigns on all of that big boss dough that he had been stacking up over the years.

Hell, they might as well enjoy it.

The two men in place to take the fall had been taken into custody already and from the looks of it, Silas and Grant had gotten off scotch free.

"Hey my favorite sister-in-law," Grant said and reached out to me for a hug.

My body tensed and I caught a glimpse of Josephine who looked at me as though I was acting strange.

I avoided eye contact with her and stared at Grant.

He smiled at me as though nothing was wrong and as though I was still oblivious to whom he had been.

I took a quick glance in Silas's and Horizon's direction, and of course he was staring at me too.

It was as though he was awaiting my next move or as though he was advising me not to bring up the hotel.

But I was going to say something as soon as I got the chance to.

It just wouldn't be right if I didn't.

I wasn't going to say anything to Josephine, but I was definitely going to give Grant an ear full.

Cursing him out was the least that I could do.

I placed on a painted smile for the rest of the evening and actually managed to enjoy myself.

The food, the laughter and even Silas and I had a few moments that I wasn't expecting.

It definitely made me think.

Did I really want to give this up?

I was sure that love would come eventually if I walked away from him, if I could, but who was to say when love would decide to come my way again?

Maybe I could stay.

After all, I had to remind myself that I had far worse secrets than he did.

He still didn't even know the half of what was hidden in my past and in my heart.

I guess the main thing was that he'd allowed me to be used for so long without coming to my rescue.

He had no idea what I'd had to do or go through for some of that money.

The humiliation and the disrespect.

The low down dirty, degrading and disgusting things that some of the clients had me do to them, were just too much for words.

He just had no idea.

And basically he did nothing about it.

To me, it was just as bad as though he'd sat there and watched.

And it pissed me off to think that he had the power to put a stop to it and he didn't.

It was just so messed up.

But to be honest, I could get over it.

If I really wanted to, I was sure that I could. I was just built that way.

But was it worth it?

Grant headed down the hall to the bathroom as everyone else made their way into the living room for a movie.

I lingered around until I heard the toilet flush and headed down the hallway.

I startled him as he opened the door.

"Envy," he said innocently.

He always seemed so innocent and so sweet.

And least he pretended to be.

And I wanted to smack the hell out of him too.

"Cut the innocent bull crap Grant. How could you? You're like a brother to me. How could you not tell me or make a way for me to get out of it? How could you?" I whined.

Grant smiled.

This fool literally smiled as though it wasn't as serious as I was making it out to be or as though the situation was amusing or funny.

"Envy, it was just business. Nothing personal. And you made us a lot of money," he said.

What?

Did he really just say that?

"Maybe that came out wrong. You decided to take the position so I could only assume that you needed the money. Well that was before you snagged Silas. But I wasn't at liberty to say anything, to anybody. Well, at least not the whole truth. It was all about the money. Everything is always about the money Envy. That's just the way that it is. But it's all over. You're free. I'm free. Silas is free. Maybe you should be grateful like we are and move on with your life. Enjoy your money. Enjoy your daughter. Just enjoy your life," Grant said.

That was the most I'd ever heard him talk, and I wasn't exaggerating.

I didn't know how to feel at that moment.

He should have told me.

Both of them should have told me.

But Grant's words were ringing in my ears.

As he'd said, it was all over.

I'd earned my freedom, and they'd paid for theirs, so starting fresh sounded like the best thing for me to do.

"Um, and what's going on here?" Josephine asked.

She folded her arms across her chest.

I looked at her and the expression on my face must have said it all because what little *sass* she did have, disappeared almost instantly.

She and Grant headed back towards the living room and I headed towards the bedroom.

I sat on the bed and checked my phone.

I had a few calls from cousins and other family, and a number or two that I didn't recognize, but I threw the phone down and just stared out our bedroom window.

I knew that Silas would be coming to see what I was up to soon so I got straight to my thoughts of him.

The bad thing was that it was hard to imagine life without him.

I guess it was because I'd spent over a year imagining forever with him, that it just didn't feel right to have to think about how life was going to be without him by my side.

I wasn't as upset as I had been.

As the days went by, the less I seemed to dwell on Silas and his deceit.

With all of my secrets, not to mention sleeping with Nolan right under Silas's nose, I'd done plenty to him too.

I'd lied to him just as much as he'd lied to me.

And I couldn't forget that there were a ton of things that he still didn't know.

So why was I really holding it against him?

If he'd told me the truth from the beginning, he was right, I wouldn't have given him the time of day.

But I had to stop trying to fool myself.

Silas was everything I'd ever wanted and needed.

He'd been good to me and good to my daughter.

What more could a woman ask for?

Just as I'd thought, a few minutes later, Silas came into the bedroom and sat down beside me.

"Your sister noticed that you weren't wearing your ring and asked if there was trouble in paradise."

I hadn't worn the ring in so long that I didn't even know where it was.

Hell I should have taken it to the pawn shop since he'd taken all of my money, but I hadn't seen it in a while.

Just as the last thought crossed my mind, he pulled out another one, a bigger one, out of his pocket.

It was the ring fit for a queen; one that his money could have afforded from the start had he not been trying to hide who he really was.

"Let me see your finger," he ordered.

He had been a lot more aggressive lately so I did what he said.

I wasn't scared of him, but I recognized that I really didn't know him or what he was capable of.

Through other conversations, he'd definitely hinted at the fact that he just might seriously hurt me if I really tried to leave him.

It was the way he said it and the look that he had in his eyes while he was saying it.

Mama hadn't raised no fool.

So, I let him put the ring on my finger.

Plus, with the pawn shop idea still on my mind, I definitely knew what I would do with it if I needed to.

Silas still hadn't given me my money back or even hinted as to where it might be.

I'd searched the house from top to bottom plenty of times, and it wasn't there.

He must've taken it somewhere.

And I had a feeling that he really wouldn't give it back unless I really gave us another shot and even then he probably wouldn't.

So, the year plus that I'd spent on the thirteenth floor had been for nothing.

I stared at the ring on my finger and then back at Silas.

At the end of the day, life doesn't get any better than what it was with him.

Or what it could be with him I should say.

With all of the lies on the table, most of them anyway, maybe we could get past it.

"I slept with Nolan," I said to him.

I don't know why I said it, but it just came out.

Maybe I wanted to hurt him.

Or maybe it was that I felt that if we were going to start over, that was something that he needed to know.

"I know. I paid him to go away."

What?

What did he just say?

"What did you say Silas? You paid who?"

"I paid Nolan to go away. It was all a set up. I'd put his fake husband on the thirteenth floor so that he could order you. I gave him the whole gay, jealous husband angle. They aren't married. The man is actually one of Nolan's family members, or maybe he was in a relationship with a family member. I can't really remember. But I paid him to pretend and paid Nolan to go away. I knew you were sleeping with him. A blind man could see it, not to mention all of the flirting at Horizon's birthday party that time. So, I approached him with the proposition, money, and told him to disappear. I paid them both up front. The only thing about it was that I had no idea that he was going to try to take the baby. He'd agreed to let you have him. He wasn't supposed to keep him. He was just supposed to disappear. We were to keep the baby and he was supposed to just vanish. But he hadn't kept his word. After that, I wanted to *take care* of him in my way, but it was too close to home, so I couldn't do anything but to try to get you legal help on the matter. I'd even managed to get him on the phone once. Nolan argued that he kept his end of the deal by leaving you alone, but he refused to give back the baby. And then, suddenly, the baby just up and passed away. He hadn't lied about the baby's death. The reports showed that everything was the truth. The coroner on the scene is a personal friend. But that's what happened. I just didn't want him to take you away from me."

I stared at Silas.

I didn't know what to feel about everything he'd just said, but I'd been right about one thing.

Nolan wasn't gay!

I knew it!

There was just no way that he could have been. Everything had been set up and played to the tee.

From the thirteenth floor visit, to the restaurant pop-up, and all the way to Nolan's behavior before stealing the baby; it had all been planned.

Everything and everyone had played their part so well.

And like everything else, Silas had been the master mind behind it all.

And Nolan taking the baby hadn't been a part of the plan, but I'd always known that it was his way to get back at me.

Bastard!

But I was confused about one thing, and instead of biting my tongue, I asked Silas about it.

"Nolan made a comment at the gravesite. He'd said that taking the baby was "his" idea. But you said that you didn't include the baby in the plan right?"

"Right. Maybe he was trying to say that the plan to disappear was "his" plan. Referring to me of course, but you took it as pertaining to the baby. I wanted the baby. I never would have wanted him to take him. I'd always wanted a son and he was the closest thing to it," Silas said.

I took a deep breath.

Well, I definitely wasn't going to start thinking about my nephew.

I already had enough on my mind and I didn't have time to be caught up in my emotions.

We chatted for a few minutes more and by the end of the conversation, I'd agreed that maybe giving things another try wouldn't be so bad.

I'd already lost everything so…what else did I have left to lose?

****

Chapter THREE

It was Valentine's Day, and I have to admit that Silas had been laying it on pretty thick.

The whole house was filled will long stemmed, red roses and balloons that he'd had delivered and not to mention the diamond earrings, necklace and bracelet set that had been waiting for me when I woke up this morning.

He'd said that he had a few errands to run, so I was home, with Horizon, answering the door every thirty minutes to receive new roses and balloon deliveries.

It had been about two months now since everything had taken place at the hotel and since I'd found out the truth about Silas.

Day by day, things were returning back to normal and half of the time I would forget that I was supposed to be making him work for it and taking things very, very slow.

We were learning to trust each other all over again and he didn't pressure me for sex.

I was definitely overdue and I figured that he was probably going insane, internally, sexually, but he didn't show it.

I'd been following the news with the hotel and had even run into one of the previous *executive* maids.

She'd been told that she was probably going to get off with probation for a few years since she didn't have any prior convictions or history of trouble. And she said that she was also going to have to pay one hell of a fine.

She'd also explained how she'd been interrogated for hours about information concerning the things at the hotel and the head men in charge.

Of course I played along as though I'd gone through the same thing. She didn't seem suspicious or anything so, I was sure that she had no idea that I was involved with bringing down the thirteenth floor.

I'd also been following the news, I'd seen quite bit on the two gentleman taking the fall and even information on celebrities and people of power that had received charges.

Their wives were divorcing them left and right, and they were being kicked off of teams, losing contracts, getting fired, and the whole nine yards.

They mentioned that they were still looking for more people involved with thirteenth floor business from the hotel but had yet to make any more arrests.

I'd already known that I hadn't gotten them information on everyone involved. I had left plenty of papers behind and by the time that they'd gone in to make the arrests and since Carmen had known that something was soon to come, she'd completely cleaned out her office.

There wasn't a piece of paper in sight when the arrests were made.

So, some of those clients and sponsors had better considered themselves lucky, because they too had dodged a bullet.

But the one person that I hadn't heard or seen anything about was Carmen.

And that just couldn't be a good thing.

The doorbell ranged and I headed towards it with a smile on my face.

What the hell were we going to do with all of these balloons and flowers?

I opened the door expecting to see a flower man but instead there was no one there---just a box.

I looked around but didn't see anyone running away or even a car passing by, so I grabbed the box, and hurriedly went back into the house, locking the front door behind me.

I peeked out of the window, just to see if someone would appear, but they didn't.

I headed back into the living room to join Horizon.

She was watching TV and singing along to the cartoons, so I sat on the couch with the box.

It was beautifully decorated, and I could only assume that it was from Silas.

I smiled at the tag that said "Open" with a smiley face.

Eager to see what was inside, I ripped off the wrapping paper and opened the box.

Confused, I picked up the pictures.

They were pictures of Silas and a man.

No, they weren't doing anything inappropriate or anything.

Thank Goodness.

But it seemed as though they had been having some kind of meeting, conversation or something.

They were sitting, talking, and then shaking hands on a few of them.

Apparently someone had been looking on and taking the photos.

Hmm, I wondered if this box was intended for me or for Silas.

Immediately I wondered who had taken them.

Who was the man in the photos with him?

And who had them delivered to our home?

I took the photos and the box to our bedroom.

I hid the photos in one of my many purses and then destroyed the box.

I didn't know what the photos meant or if they were meant for me to see them at all, but something in me told me to keep them.

If Silas was expecting them, he would have to ask me for them, and then I could question him about them.

The doorbell ranged again, and I headed back to the living room.

This time it actually was the flower man, but instead of the roses being red, this time they were white.

I accepted them and then read the tag attached to them.

I frowned immediately.

These roses weren't for me at all.

They were for Silas.

And they were from Carmen.

Was she out of jail?

And why was she sending Silas flowers?

Angry, I called Silas's phone but just as the phone started to ring, he walked through the front door.

I reached him the flowers and then folded my arms across my chest.

He looked at them and then read the tag aloud.

The tag had the number 713 written on it.

I knew that it meant something so I waited for him to explain.

"713 means that the police aren't as convinced as they should be. It doesn't mean that they are on to us or anything, but it does mean that they are still asking questions and still looking for whatever they could find. But it's nothing to worry about. The sponsors and clients definitely don't know much of anything. The men won't fold and neither will Carmen. The men and Carmen owe me everything. Everything will be fine," Silas assured me as he headed to the trashcan and tossed the flowers inside.

I didn't like that he said things that couldn't exactly be explained.

He said just enough and I knew that I didn't have a choice but to take it for what it was.

But if Carmen knew all of this, I could only hope and assume that maybe she was still in jail too.

Maybe her little plan to get off on the charges hadn't worked after all.

I really hoped that they didn't.

With Carmen out of sight and out of mind, I could truly see the difference in my relationship with Silas.

She had definitely been a problem and I was hoping that the problem was gone, and hopefully gone for good.

Or a few years at least.

Silas handed me the bags that he'd been carrying, told me to get Horizon ready, and then told me to be dressed when he got back home.

I hadn't asked where he was taking her.

Knowing him, he had already worked things out with Josephine and was probably meeting her half way so that her oldest daughter could babysit.

I knew that he had something special planned so I tried to forget about the roses, the pictures, and Carmen, and headed to get myself together.

The all white dress that Silas had purchased was so tight that I could barely move.

But I liked it.

It hugged my body in all of the right places and my hips and my booty looked bigger than ever.

Silas ordered me to put on the diamonds that he'd given to me as a gift that morning and the Louboutin all white, red bottom pumps, sprinkled with diamonds and rhinestones, made me look better than the woman of any man's wet dream.

I looked damn good.

Looking at myself in the mirror, reality whispered in my ear.

This is what my life was going to be like with Silas.

This was my future.

A life that I'd never so much as imagined was in the palm of my hand.

I would be a fool not to let the past go and move forward.

And because of the things that I'd done in my past, it was only right.

Silas returned all of two hours later.

I was surprised to see that he was already dressed when he enter the house.

He was wearing an all-white suit, and looked as sharp as a razor blade.

"You ready?"

I smiled and nodded my head as he reached for my hand.

We headed out the door to the all-white, stretched Hummer limousine.

I entered it to see that it was also full of red roses and what had to be a hundred gift boxes and bags.

I smiled at him and felt like a kid in a candy store.

Once Silas was settled beside of me, I kissed him.

I kissed him because I still loved him.

I kissed him because he'd always been good to me, despite not saving me from the hotel.

I kissed him because I knew that I would never meet anyone else like him and I was positive that no one would ever truly want me as much as he did.

But most of all, I kissed him because at that very moment, I truly, and fully, decided to forgive him.

We rode for a little while until we came to a boat dock.

I got out and Silas led me towards a boat.

As we walked, women in all-white as well, were lined up and they each handed me a single rose along the way, until we were directly in front of a big white boat with green letters.

I smiled as I noticed that the boat's name was "Horizon".

"This is another one of your gifts. This boat is yours. Not mine. Not ours. But yours." Silas said.

I kissed him again and took a deep breath as we got onto the boat.

As soon as my feet touched the floor of "Horizon", immediately the pampering began.

For the next few hours the boat took us far away from the world while we enjoyed each other's company.

I can't really describe what it was that I was feeling.

I was overwhelmed.

I was filled with joy.

Happy.

Yes, that one word described it all.

I felt happy.

"I love you so much Envy. You are the apple of my eye," Silas said as a waiter appeared and handed me a fake white apple.

I looked at it as Silas waited for me to figure out how to open it.

Once I did, I saw the fake apple open up and there was a key inside.

"This is the key to my heart, and it is yours forever. Our and it's also the key to your new white Porsche," Silas said.

I started to blush but I knew that he wasn't done.

"I love you because you are genuine and caring. And because you're as sweet as can be, most of the time," Silas laughed as another waiter brought me a box of strawberries that had been dipped in white chocolate.

"But most of all, whether you know it or not, I love you because you have changed my life. And you have truly given me something to live for. You are my angel," Silas said, as one more waiter carried a big box over to me.

I opened it to find that it was a white angel; but it was more like a picture frame. It had spaces for individual pictures and each of them already had a picture inside of them. A picture of Silas, Horizon and I were in the slot directly in the middle, and all around it, there were pictures of my family; of my parents, all of my sisters, my nieces and nephews, including Tia's son that had passed away.

My heart started to melt and I wondered how he had gotten some of the photos. Some of them I had never seen, so he must have taken them on his own.

And some of them should have been burned down with the house, but I was sure that maybe he'd thought to get them out prior to, and just hadn't said anything.

The gift really touched my heart and I couldn't do anything but look at Silas with love.

Things like this is why he'd gotten me, and these were the same type of things that were also going to ensure that he was able to keep me.

Who would do all of this if they didn't really love someone?

Who would go to such extremes if they really didn't care about the person?

I was convinced.

Even though our definition of love may not have been the same and even though I would have liked to have thought that I would have done things differently had the shoe been on the other foot, as much as he knew how to, and to the best of his ability, I was sure that Silas loved me.

And no one could ever tell me anything different.

We continued to sail as we made our way to the bottom level of the boat, where a bed was waiting for us.

And for the first time in what seemed like forever, we made love.

And oh how good it was!

***

"You look beautiful!" I squealed as Josephine covered her face with the veil.

It was the day of her wedding renewal, which was also the day of her wedding anniversary.

Seeing her made me remember just how much I wanted to be Silas's wife.

Though the wedding date had been pushed back, I wanted so desperately to have my turn to stand at the altar and say I do.

But seeing as to how things were going great between Silas and I, we should be back on the road towards marriage pretty soon.

Yes, I'd forgiven him, but I just wanted to make sure everything was in the clear.

We never so much as mentioned the hotel to each other these days, and we were pretty much walking around as though none of it had ever happened.

But you could never be too sure of the future and just in case everything from all angles weren't as peachy as they seemed, it was best that we waited for a while before making such a huge decision.

"Let's do this, Josephine said.

I stared at the outside ceremony space.

It was beautiful.

The colors, the flowers, everything was just beautiful.

The reception space was only a few feet over and it looked just as exquisite.

Everything was ready.

The food smelled amazing.

The tables, with the little "Reserved" note cards looked lovely.

It was the perfect day for a wedding.

Minutes later, I was walking my sister down the created space referred to as the aisle.

Josephine was crying and I couldn't help but cry too.

People these days barely stayed married a year, but they had made it darn near a lifetime together.

Through ups and downs, affairs and *pimping*, they'd made it.

And for the first time ever, I, Envy, was envious of something.

But it was all love.

I took my place beside her as she took Grant's hand.

They looked at each other as though nothing else in the world mattered.

I smiled as one of our cousins started to sing and I couldn't help but become overwhelmed.

I couldn't wait for my turn and it was coming soon.

It was coming very soon.

But before the only part of the wedding that actually mattered could begin…it was over.

So many shots were fired that I lost count.

I fell to the ground in a hurry and full of terror.

Instinctively, I started to slide around on the ground looking for Horizon.

I didn't see her so I started to panic, but because the shooting continued, I was forced to lie still, and search for her with my eyes.

Finally I spotted her…and Silas.

Silas was lying over her, shielding her.

I couldn't believe that he'd made it to where she had been standing as a flower girl, from where he'd been standing as a groomsman.

But there he was, shielding my baby as thought he was her guardian angel.

Oh thank the Man above for him!

Finally, the shooting stopped and it seemed as though no one moved for what felt like eternity.

I wondered if everyone was dead or if they were as afraid to move as I was.

Did that just happen?

A drive-by?

At a wedding?

Who does that?

"Envy!" Silas's yell startled me.

He was alive.

I was still frozen as I watched Silas and Horizon stand to their feet, and head in my direction.

It seemed as though everyone else followed Silas's actions and those that could get up from the ground, stood.

As Silas helped me up, I looked for Josephine.

I could only see the bottom of her dress being as to the fact that Grant must have dived on top of her as well.

Silas followed my eyes and together we headed to them to assist.

I could hear Josephine crying before I could even see her face.

Horizon was crying too, so I picked her up.

"Grant?" Silas shook him but he didn't say anything.

Josephine cried even louder and started to call my name.

Silas moved Grant off of her and her cries filled the atmosphere and everyone else as well as myself, started to cry too.

Looking around, a few family members, servers and friends had been shot, but none seemed to be fatal.

Josephine reached for my hand and that's when I saw the blood.

Placing Horizon in a chair and with the sirens wailing in the distance, I helped Josephine to her feet.

"He saved me. He jumped in front of the bullet. He took a bullet for me," Josephine cried.

I looked at Silas who was looking at the single gunshot wound to the back of Grant's head.

I could tell by the look on Silas's face that he felt like dying.

Or maybe he felt like crying.

Or both I supposed.

He held Grant's head close to his chest as though he was a hit dog.

Though they were always cordial before I found out the truth about them, Silas didn't try to hide the love that he felt for his friend at that moment.

He didn't make any noise but finally the tears started to flow endlessly from his eyes.

My heart broke for him and for Josephine and I wanted to comfort them both but Josephine needed me more as she started to break down.

Out of nowhere, it started to rain, and it seemed to only make things worse.

Everyone seemed to cry louder and started to run around in a panic.

Help finally arrived and the emergency crew rushed over to Silas and tried to help Grant but Silas would let him go.

They pulled and pulled, but Silas wouldn't let go.

"Silas," I called out to him.

At the sound of my voice, he let him go.

The workers went to work and started to probe over Grant.

Horizon wanted Josephine to pick her up, so she did and I made my way over to Silas.

I hugged him but he didn't hug me back.

He just sat there.

But then…

"Get him up! Let's go! He still has a pulse!"

Oh thank goodness!

***

"Doctors said that it's a miracle that he survived. He doesn't remember anything or anyone. He's pretty much like a small child. Only thing is, he'll be like that forever. He won't advance or get better, but he's still alive. They said he will make some noises and maybe even movement, but the damage to his brain won't allow him to learn to talk, or walk, or do anything like that again. And they said if so, it won't be much," Josephine said.

It had only been a little over a week since the wedding shooting.

Two family friends were able to describe the car, but no one saw the shooters.

As many shots being fired, we were sure that there were a few of them but no one had been lucky enough to catch a glimpse.

Seven people were injured; Grant's head wound being the worst of them.

Josephine explained that had not Grant jumped in front of her when he did, she would have surely been shot right in the face.

She said that he'd looked her straight in the eyes as the bullet struck him, as though he'd wanted to get one last look at her.

As though he wanted her to know that he loved her enough to die for her.

The saddest, yet sweetest thing I'd ever heard in my entire life.

Though Grant was pretty much going to be helpless for the rest of his life, Josephine vowed that she would never leave his side.

She'd said that she would take care of him forever and even after that if she could.

I was still freaked out by it all.

I just didn't know who would do something so cruel, to Josephine that is.

They had to have known that the wedding was taking place on that date and at that time.

They had to be someone that knows Josephine.

Or Grant.

Hanging up with Josephine, I continued to think.

Yeah, I was sure that it had nothing to do with Josephine and everything to do with Grant and who he had been or something to that extent.

As for Silas, he still wasn't exactly himself.

I wasn't sure if he was in shock or if it was the realization that even though his best friend wasn't physically dead---everything and every memory of their friendship was gone.

He was quiet most days and some days he forced himself to be there for Horizon and I, but I could see that he was hurting.

He was always on the go so I was also sure that he was doing everything within his power to find out who was responsible for the shooting.

He wanted them and he wanted them bad.

I could feel it.

As for me, I was okay I suppose.

I'd been through worse.

I just hated to see so many people that I loved hurting.

Putting Horizon down for a nap and after calling to check on Silas, I headed to relax but a knock at the door told me that I wasn't going to be relaxing anytime soon.

I opened the door and opened my mouth at the same time.

There she was, in the flesh…

Carmen.

****

Chapter FOUR

"Yeah, bitch, I'm back," she said with a smirk on her face.

Immediately, I became guarded and prepared myself for anything.

"What are you doing here Carmen? Aren't you supposed to be in jail or something?"

"Nope. Actually I'm supposed to be locked away and high on medication, but that's neither here nor there. I need to speak with Silas. I called his phone, but he didn't answer or call me back. He always calls me back, so something is wrong," she said.

I guess Silas was telling the truth about her buying her way out of the mental institution.

And her mentioning that she knew something was wrong with Silas, low-key pissed me off.

It disturbed me that she knew him a lot better than I preferred.

Something was wrong, but that was none of her business.

"Carmen, leave, and don't come back to my house again," I said and attempted to shut the door, but she stopped it with her hand.

"Let me make something clear. It's because of me that you are still in this house and that the police didn't come after everything that you and Silas have. Sure, your snitching kept you out of jail, at least that's the promise that the detective made to you I'm sure. But there is someone over his head. And someone over their head. And that someone is more than likely on my payroll. So, you should be saying thank you. But I'll make sure that Silas thanks me enough for the both of you," Carmen said and turned to walk away but something took over me.

I was tired of her ass and it was time that I showed her just how tired I was.

I balled up my fists and punched her with all of my might in the back of her head.

But to my surprise, it was as though she was expecting it, because the blow that she swing my way took me by surprised, and hit me dead in the eye.

And from that moment, it was on!

I punched her, she punched me, and for another minute or so, we fought each other as though our lives depended on it.

Carmen got ahold of my hair and tried to take me down to the ground but I managed to get a hand full of hers and I brought her down with me.

On top, I was about to go in on her and beat her for everything that she had ever done to me, but before I could even get started, Silas came out of nowhere, snatched me up with one hand, and controlled Carmen with his other.

I was in frenzy and we'd caused such a ruckus that we'd woken up Horizon and she was standing there, watching and crying.

And though I felt bad for behaving that way in front of her, I wanted Carmen's ass, again, and I wanted it bad!

"Envy, sit your ass down, now!" Silas yelled.

I looked at him confused.

Was he taking her side?

"Both of you should be ashamed. Two grown ass women carrying on like little girls. Whether the both of you like it or not, we need each other in a way. We are here because we all played a part, cut some deals and pulled a few strings to ensure that we remained free. You may not like it, but you both better figure out what the hell you are going to do about it because this whole investigation thing is far from over. I know how the law operates, and if there is any doubt, any tiny thing that might not make sense, they will follow it. And with Carmen pretty much walking on all of the charges, I'm sure that there are going to be eyes on her; which means there are going to be eyes on me because we still have unfinished business. So Envy that means that there is going to be eyes on you too. So both of you, chill, damn," Silas concluded, grabbed Horizon by the hand and walked away.

I wondered what unfinished business they had to take care of, but I knew that it would be a waste of time for me to even ask.

"Bitch."

"Slut."

"Die."

"Not before you do," Carmen said, fixed her clothes, placed on her sunglasses and walked away.

What the hell did she mean by that?

I didn't take anything that she said lightly.

I would be a fool to.

Still upset, I started to pace back and forth.

"Envy, you can't let Carmen get to you. Soon she will be out of our lives forever. In the meantime, let me handle her. She's powerful and she's mentally unstable. I know her, but she's also sneaky. I never know what she just might do. She has just as many connections and strings as I do, and she doesn't mind using them to get the job done. But she knows that I will hurt her over you, so you don't have to go around trying to fight her over me. She will never have me. I'm yours. Everything will be fine. I got you," Silas said once Carmen was gone and though I believed him, in a way I felt that it wasn't enough.

I was tired of dealing with Carmen.

I wanted her out of my life!

What was so hard about that?

"I'm sure she has other copies of paperwork and everything else. I'm sure she's still holding on to documentation with the truth about Grant and I and as for you, well, I just don't want her to do anything to you. Just let me handle her. I'm the only one that can handle her. Put some ice on that eye."

He asked Horizon if she wanted to go get ice cream and immediately her frown turned upside down. I tried to hug her but she moved from within my reach, grabbed Silas's hand and they headed out the door.

Aw, I scared my munchkin.

I hated that Horizon had to see me out of character like that, which made me hate Carmen even more.

I headed to check on my eye.

It was swelling pretty fast and starting to turn colors.

She'd gotten me good, but I was going to get her back if it was the last thing that I do.

I wasn't scared of her and I wasn't going to live my life in fear no matter how much power she had.

It was time that I started protecting myself from everybody, including Silas.

You know, just in case.

***

"Let's run off and get married. I love you. What are we really waiting for? And besides, if something happens to me, I want you to have everything and have access to all of my accounts, stocks and all assets, legally," Silas said.

I looked at him.

What is he talking about?

Was something going to happen to him?

"I mean, we saw what happened to Grant, just like that, and we just have to be prepared. I'm coming to terms that because of the lifestyle that I have lived, I'm sure that I have an enemy or two out there somewhere. I want you and Horizon to be set for life."

"Well, if you gave my money back we would be fine, if something happened to you," I said reminding him that he hadn't mentioned it, though we were on good terms.

"You would be fine for a while. But not forever. I had it counted. It's a good bit, for you, but it would be gone in a year or two, unless you invested it into something. But I have more than enough. Let's get married. Besides, it'll piss off Carmen," Silas smiled.

Now, he was talking my kind of language!

Boy did I like the sound of that!

Wait a minute.

She's crazy remember, so maybe pissing her off isn't such a good thing.

"Don't worry. She would try some slick shit, but she also fears the fact that I would hate her. It's just how she thinks, and I know how she thinks. But we can't worry about Carmen. We can only worry about us. Florida has the perfect little destination wedding and honeymoon package. You wanna take a chance with me?" Silas said.

Hmm…I thought I already was.

But considering everything that had gone on and what Silas had said, maybe he was right.

We could be here one day and gone the next.

I'd long since forgiven him, so what were we really waiting around for?

You know what, no more over thinking things.

"Yes. Let's do it. When?"

"Now," Silas said and got up from the couch and got his keys," and waited for Horizon and I to follow.

"We need to pack," I smiled.

"We will buy along the way. We have plenty of money to waste," he said and with that out the door we went.

I was smiling bigger and brighter than ever before.

I was getting married…finally!

***

"How are you?" Nolan asked.

We were still in Key West, Florida.

Silas and I had gotten married the day before and he and Horizon were still on the beach.

I'd come up to the room to relax a little and just my luck, I ran into Nolan.

I just looked at him.

I didn't exactly know what to feel, but I knew that for his sake, he had better turn around and walk away.

"So you finally tied the knot huh?" Nolan asked nodding at my hand.

What was he doing here?

"I don't have anything to say to you," I said and attempted to go into my room and shut the door but Nolan pushed his way in behind me.

"Nolan get out!"

"Do you know how hard it was for me to stand there and watch you marry him?"

What?

"Yes, I followed you here. I never stopped loving you. I never stopped watching you. I have to make sure that you're safe," Nolan said.

I looked at him as if he was insane, when in reality, he kind of was.

What was he doing watching me?

And I sure as hell didn't need his protection.

"Nolan please. Dismiss me with the bull crap, okay. You can be bought just like everybody else," I said with an attitude, and grabbed my phone, but Nolan snatched it out of my hand.

"I needed the money. The funeral and bills left behind had me in debt. And the baby. He offered the money, and I needed it. But by then, I was already in love with you Envy. I wanted to be with you," Nolan said.

"Nolan, whether he paid you or not, I didn't love you and eventually I would have stopped sleeping with you. What we were doing was wrong and no matter what you thought we had, all we had was sex. It was wrong and disrespectful to my sister. We both know that we'd crossed the line. And let's not even bring up you taking the baby from me. A while ago, you would have been in danger just being this close to me, but I'm in a better place now and I believe that everything happens for a reason. Good and bad."

"Sometimes, but other times things don't just happen. They can be forced," Nolan said.

What the hell did he mean by that?

"Look all I'm saying is he came to visit that day to try to convince me to give you the baby back. I'd moved and everything, so I don't know how he found me. But he wasn't upset. All he'd said was that he wanted to make you happy. He even offered me more money but I told him that I needed him. I needed the baby more than you thought that I did. I guess he could understand since he went into a rant about losing his own daughter. I could see that he truly loved his child and the pain from losing her was the only thing that helped him understand where I was coming from. He asked to see him. He went to look in on the baby while he took a nap and then he left. All I'm saying is the baby never woke up after that. I went in only a few minutes later to wake him up to feed him, and he was gone. The reports said SIDS but something just didn't seem right to me. Had Silas not noticed that he wasn't breathing when he'd gone in to see him? Or was I supposed to believe that my son took his last breath only minutes after? But hey, what do I know," Nolan said.

What?

Was he trying to say that Silas killed the baby?

And so Silas knew where Nolan was all along and had actually gone to see the baby the day of his death?

No, he would have told me.

Silas did mention that he'd spoken to Nolan; but he hadn't said anything about seeing him.

No, Silas wouldn't have done anything to harm the baby.

It just had to be a coincidence.

"Nolan, what are you trying to say?"

"I'm not saying anything. I just found it odd, that's all. After all, how well can you truly know a person or know what their capable of? The baby was just fine before he came. But he's gone now, so enough about that. I'm here for you. I would have never left you Envy. I shouldn't have taken the money."

"Nolan, get out okay. You're still not hearing me. There was nothing there. Nothing but sex. I love Silas. The whole time, I loved Silas. Please just leave," I said and reached for my phone again, but he moved his hand.

Nolan came closer to me.

"I came here for you and I'm not leaving here without you," Nolan said.

"I'm married to Silas and even if I wasn't, you could never have any other part of me again," I said and tried to grab my phone again.

"You wanna bet," Nolan said, as he pushed me down on the bed and started to pull at my swim suit and cover up.

"Move! Nolan! Get the hell off of me!" I yelled and swatted at him but he placed all of his weight on me.

At the sound of him ripping the bottom half of my swim suit off, I fought even harder.

Nolan choked me as he freed himself, all the while taking blow after blow to the chest and face.

But no matter what I did, he didn't stop.

He just didn't stop.

No, this could not be happening!

Silas I need your help!

He'd begged me to stay a little while longer on the beach but I was so tired from giving him the *business* all night that I just wanted to come back into the room and relax.

"I can't breathe. Get off of me, I can't breathe!" I managed to get out as I gasped for air and then I felt it.

I felt Nolan's dick inside of me.

He entered me forcefully, and just sat there for a second to taunt me.

He continued to choke me as he started to stroke.

Somebody, anybody, please help me!

But no one came.

No one came to help me.

Where was my husband when I needed him the most?

He promised to protect me.

He promised to keep me safe.

But where was he now?

He wasn't there to save me the one time I needed him more than ever.

Feeling like I was about to pass out, finally, I stopped fighting Nolan and just laid there.

The more Nolan pumped away inside of me, the more I wanted to just roll over and die.

It seemed as though with each pump, I lost a piece of who I used to be.

He was raping me.

He was really raping me.

My mind didn't want to accept it, but my body forced my brain to believe it, because it was true.

I'd had close encounters before, but no one had ever succeeded.

No one but Nolan.

How could he?

Why would he?

Little did he know, he'd might as well have considered himself dead.

He was a dead man.

And I was going to make sure of that.

Maybe Silas being who he was wasn't so bad after all.

It seemed like forever, but finally he released himself inside of me.

He completely let go of my throat and stood to his feet.

"Now get your shit, and let's go. Like I said, I'm not leaving here without you," Nolan said.

I didn't look at him.

I didn't do anything.

I didn't cry.

I didn't move.

And it seemed as though I barely even breathed.

I just laid there.

I just couldn't believe what had just happened to me.

He wouldn't get away with this.

He wouldn't get away with what he'd done to me.

Becoming impatient, Nolan started to pull at my legs.

"Okay! Get the hell off of me!" I said finally and kicked at him so that he would stop pulling me.

"Let's go Envy…now," he said and pulled out a gun.

Immediately seeing the gun, I thought about the shooting at Josephine's wedding.

I don't know why, but it was as though something deep inside my heart told me that just maybe…

He did say that he had been following me.

I just had to ask.

Something just told me to ask.

"Were you responsible for the shooting at Josephine's wedding?" I asked Nolan.

"Well since you asked, yes. I thought that it was your wedding. I was trying to stop your wedding. I'd seen you and Josephine at the wedding shops a few times, and when I followed you to the ceremony site and saw that it was decorated, I assumed that it was your wedding. I knew that your sister was already married, so that only left you. Silas didn't deserve you. I deserved you. It was a sudden decision, but I had to do something. So, I made a few calls, offered a few dollars, since Silas had paid me more than enough, to a few young thugs. They were only supposed to shoot the place up before the ceremony actually started. I figured it would ruin the day and maybe you would see it as a sign. But they were late to the job. Nobody was supposed to get hurt. I just wanted them to stop the wedding. I just wanted to stop the show. I watched it on the news and found out that I'd made a mistake. I saw your sister crying about what had happened to her husband on the news and I knew then that I'd been wrong. So, I still drove by you house and followed you when I could. The day that you guys decided to take this long drive here, I had just pulled up to sit for a while, and then I saw y'all come out. I followed you to the store to get gas. You looked right in my direction while you went in the store, but you didn't see me. When I saw you come out with bags full of snacks, I knew that something was up so I got out and hurriedly pumped what I could in gas so that I could be ready to take off behind you guys. I followed y'all all the way here. I thought it was just a vacation. Hell, I needed one of those for myself. I checked in right behind after y'all, and told them that I wanted to be on the same floor as my brother and sister-in-law, who had just gotten a room right before me. I gave your names, and though I'm sure they weren't supposed to, that placed me right next door. I was only supposed to sleep for a few hours and figured that y'all would be trying to sleep too considering the long drive. Once I woke up later on in the evening and as I took a stroll on the beach, imagine my surprise to see you and Silas under a gazebo, with a man holding a bible. At the sight of the kiss, I knew that I was too late and it was already done. You were already married. But it's not over yet. It's not over until I say it's over. Let's go," Nolan threw me a pair of shorts that were sitting on the table and I stood up to put them on.

He was behind the shooting?

He could have killed me!

He could have killed all of us, including my daughter.

And he had followed us for hours on our road trip and I do mean hours, just to see what we were up to and where we were going?

Now, it doesn't get any crazier than that!

The anger that was stirring up inside of me, told me that I was about to do something stupid and downright reckless.

And reckless and stupid was exactly what it was.

Before Nolan had time to see it coming, I punched him as hard as I could, followed it with a powerful shove and focused on the gun as it fell to the floor.

I raced to it, picked it up, and before Nolan could even react, pulled the trigger, twice, and just like that…

Nolan was gone.

Dead.

Instead of a feeling of relief or triumph, tell me why I felt just a tad bit of remorse.

What have I done?

Sure after what he'd just done to me I wanted him dead, but my plan had been to get Silas to do it.

Not me.

It was only seconds after I'd shot him, in came Silas and Horizon.

Silas stared at Nolan's body, and then at me.

"Mommy, why is Nolan on the floor? Nolan get up and where is the baby? I want to see him." Horizon said.

Of course we hadn't exactly told her about the baby passing away.

Tia getting killed right in front of her was more than a child her age was supposed to witness, so we'd just told her that the baby was with Nolan.

Of course Nolan didn't answer her and neither did I.

I looked at Silas, as he now looked at me.

I'd tried to explain but I couldn't.

I just couldn't say anything.

A knock came at the door no sooner than Silas had entered and he ordered me to take Horizon into the bathroom.

After chatting for what seemed like forever, and after answering all one million of Horizon's questions, with lies of course, Silas came into the bathroom and ordered for us to come out.

Heading over to the bed, Nolan's body, the gun, the bedsheets and my ripped bikini bottoms were all gone.

Silas turned the TV on for Horizon and we headed to the balcony to talk.

"Did he touch you?"

I nodded my head.

I still hadn't shown any kind of emotion, partly because I didn't know what to feel.

It was as though my mind still couldn't believe the last hour of my life.

Being that I'd had sex more times than ten women combined, and even had some nasty, disrespectful, degrading things done to me sexually, I'd never had anyone to successfully just *take* what was mine and not in the least bit theirs.

It was a feeling that I couldn't quite describe.

How could he do that to me?

And though I was protecting myself, and acted out of anger and rage, I still felt somewhat bad for what I'd done.

But he deserved it.

He freakin' deserved it!

Silas didn't even try to hide the fact that he was upset, as he motioned for me to enter his arms and for me to lay my head on his chest.

It wasn't until I'd heard the sound of his heartbeat that I'd started to whimper.

It all had happened so fast.

What the hell was Nolan thinking?

Why couldn't he have just left me alone like he'd been paid to do?

I was so furious!

Look what he made me do!

It was definitely self-defense, or temporary insanity, and I had the DNA to prove what had happened to me, so I wasn't exactly concerned with any legal issues, not all that much anyway.

But it still didn't change the fact of what he'd done or that I'd actually had to be the one to pull the trigger.

"Don't worry. Everything is going to be okay. I took care of everything," Silas said and I was sure that he had.

Finally allowing my emotions to run wild, Silas held me close. He held me tighter than he ever had before.

After a while, Silas cleared his throat and then he said something else.

"Oh, and by the way, he was still breathing. He wasn't dead. You didn't kill him. But he will wish that you had once I get through with him," Silas said.

Uh oh.

***

We were back in Charlotte and I was still in a funk.

This was supposed to be the happiest time of my life and all I could think about was what had happened with Nolan.

I thought about it all day and all night, and I just couldn't seem to shake it off.

Silas assured me that everything would be just fine and that I would never have to worry about Nolan again, but not even his reassurance could take away whatever it was that I was feeling inside.

I'd told Silas detail by detail what happened.

He was so angry.

Hell you would have thought that it had all happened to him.

I told him everything that Nolan had said to me; including the wedding shooting and the comments he'd made in reference to the baby's death.

Of course Silas said that he would have never harmed the baby and denied seeing the baby the day that he'd died.

He said that Nolan was lying.

But Nolan hadn't sounded like he was lying to me, but it was a possibility.

And I should have kept the part about Nolan being responsible for what had happened to Grant to myself. It had Silas wanting to kill Nolan's whole family.

But he promised that I would never have to see or hear from Nolan again.

I knew that I wouldn't, but what was I supposed to do with the memories?

I swear, after all of this, I was going to need some help. I'm talking therapy, medication, the whole nine yards.

I didn't sign up for all of this.

It seemed as though I was paying for my mistakes, over and over again.

I felt as though the weight of the world was on my shoulders.

But I couldn't blame anyone but myself for the way that my life had turned out.

If I hadn't gone up to the thirteenth floor, a lot of what had happened in my life over the last year or two wouldn't have. I mean a lot of things that had either happened or were happening in my life, would be non-existent.

And I could even take it way back and say that had I not been so caught up in playing house with a man who I'd never even gotten married to, instead of bettering myself and getting an education so that I could stand on my two feet, I wouldn't be in this situation.

I wouldn't have had to settle as a maid.

I would have never met Carmen.

I wouldn't have gotten fired for turning down the position on the thirteenth floor, which led to Tia sleeping with Nolan, getting pregnant, and getting killed by his wife.

It was because of me that my life was so screwed up.

I was broke before, but you know what, then, my life was ten times better than this.

My only problem then was paying my bills.

It seemed like such a small problem now, because now, bills were the least of my worries.

Now, I had to worry about stalkers, crazy ex-wives, avoiding jail time, and that was just half of my problems.

I guess the saying was true that you should be careful what you wish for…because you just might get it.

And it may not be what you hoped that it would be.

Pulling up at our home, immediately I spotted her car.

Carmen.

I was not in the mood for this today!

Silas damn near jumped out of the car before coming to a complete stop.

She was headed up the driveway and I could tell that she was up to no good.

After what I had just gone through, I was not going to deal with her and her stupid ass.

And if Silas couldn't understand that, well, he could hit the road and run right on back to her.

I was sure that she would take him back with opened arms.

I took my time getting out behind him.

I didn't even really care what it was that they were talking about.

I was his wife now, so what was understood, no longer had to be explained.

He was mine.

All mine.

Whether she liked it or not.

As I approached, Silas looked at her as though he was forcing her to speak to me or something.

"Oh, I'm shaking in my boots. Didn't know you had it in you, killer. Well, almost a killer. Hello Envy," Carmen said sarcastically, with a laugh as I walked towards the front door.

She was going to make me go in her mouth and this time, nothing but the Man above would be able to get me off of her.

"Bitch, don't get smacked."

"Try me."

Silas shook his head and nodded in Horizon's direction.

"Don't tempt me. And from now on, if for whatever reason you have to speak to me, and oh how I'm praying that you don't have to or maybe I should say that you won't bother to, but if for some odd reason, if you have to speak to me, you can call me Mrs. Okeke. That would be just fine, thank you," I said with a small giggle and wiggled my finger at her.

Her expression told me that she immediately noticed the band and that it had caught her by surprise, but she tried to play it off.

"Well, at least we got something in common now, Mrs. Okeke…number three," she said and reached Silas the papers that she was holding and walked away.

I waited until we were inside of the house to speak.

I didn't care what kind of business relationship they had or whatever ties that were still in between them, she wasn't going to keep bringing her ass to my house.

Period.

"What was that about?"

"She handled the paperwork for Nolan's death cover-up. He's not dead of course, but he'll never be seen again, so we had to take care of it properly. Her connections are stronger when it comes to hiding murders, staging deaths, changing identities and things of that sort. You'll probably see something on the news today that a man was found robbed and dead in an alley. Face beat beyond recognition. He will later be identified as Nolan. Don't worry, we didn't kill him. I paid for the corpse. I also paid the workers at the hotel plenty for their help and their silence. The hotel footage of us ever been there, as well as our information was destroyed. So we can just try to put it all behind us okay," Silas said.

I nodded.

Knowing who he really was, really allowed me to see what kind of things he was involved in and just what kind of things that he could actually make happen.

I was able to see what he was capable of and I was able to see how much power he had, and boy was it a lot.

And...I was also able to see Carmen's power as well.

"So you told her about Nolan, but not about the marriage?" I questioned him.

"I told her what I needed her to do. She didn't ask questions. She never does. She just does it. We didn't discuss anything other than making sure that she handled what needed to be handled," Silas said.

"What if she uses it against us one day?"

Carmen was capable of anything.

But Silas seemed to trust her with his life.

Maybe even more than he trusted me.

"She won't. There's too much dirt and too many cover-ups involved. Like I told you, you'll be fine," Silas said taking our bags to our bedroom.

I got Horizon a snack and then headed back out the front door to check the mail.

It was hot and sticky, but in a way, the sun and the birds chirping, made me feel just a little better.

But still I wondered, just what in the hell did they do with the real Nolan?

There was no telling what someone like Silas and Carmen were up to and it was probably better that I didn't ask too many questions on the matter.

I grabbed over twenty envelopes from the mail and started to go through them.

All of them were bills, except for one of them.

Instantly I recognized the handwriting.

I couldn't believe my eyes.

It was from Sonni.

My sister Sonni.

Or should I call her Savannah?

She was reaching out to me?

Why?

I opened the envelope in a hurry, and read the note that was inside.

"Meet me at the park downtown. Tomorrow. Noon."

That was it.

I read the note three more times, aloud, trying to make sense of it all.

So Sonni was back in town?

And she wanted to meet?

But the last time I saw her she'd said that she pretty much never wanted to see me or anyone else in her family again.

So why was she back?

Why did she want to meet now?

I hated to say this, but this couldn't be a good thing.

She'd faked her death to get away from us, so if she was back, I was sure that it was for a reason.

Something had to be or had to have gone wrong.

And then again, maybe somehow she missed us and she just wanted to see me.

It was a slight possibility that was the reason.

Maybe it was "Savannah" who had a problem with loving us, and not necessarily Sonni.

With Sonni on my mind, on top of everything else, I headed back into the house, eagerly anticipating tomorrow...

I spotted Sonni as soon as I entered the park.

She was sitting on a bench, watching the kids play on the swings.

Just from looking at her from a far, she appeared different.

Her hair had grown back.

Actually it was way too long, too fast, so maybe it was a long weave.

The shade of her arm was about three shades darker than when I'd last see her and though she was sitting, wearing a loose fitting white dress, I could tell that she'd put on just a little bit of weight.

I was extremely nervous.

I was nervous as to why she wanted to see me and I could only hope that it was because of the right reasons and not because of something else.

I walked towards her, took a deep breath once I reached her and tapped her on her shoulder.

"Silas you're late," Sonni said, as she turned around.

She damn near passed out when she saw that it was me.

Silas?

She was here to meet Silas?

Huh?

"Uh….Envy, um, hi," Sonni mumbled uncomfortably.

Why in the hell was she trying to meet up with Silas?

What business did she have with my husband?

"So you were expecting Silas? Not me? Why?" I questioned her.

She looked at me all funny with her weird ass.

"Why did you open his mail?" Sonni questioned.

Huh?

What kind of question is that?

"First off, he is my husband so if I want to open his mail, I'll do as I please. Secondly, your envelope was addressed to me, not Silas," I said to her.

She looked confused.

"No, it was supposed to be for Silas. Maybe you crossed my mind at the time and I put your name on it instead. I'm not sure. But I needed to see Silas…not you. I don't need to or want to see you."

You would think that her words wouldn't hurt anymore, but they did.

They hurt so bad.

"Why?"

"Envy, it has nothing to do with you. It's none of your business. Just go home," Sonni said but I grabbed her arm as she tried to walk away.

"Let go of me Envy," Sonni said angrily.

"Not until you tell me why you wanted to meet up with my husband," I yelled at her.

"Envy, again, it has nothing to do with you. This is between me and Silas. Stay out of it and out of my way," Sonni said, pulled away, and ran as fast as she could.

And I mean she actually ran as though I was going to chase her.

It was almost comical watching her run away as though she was a little baby roach and I'd stomped my foot in her direction.

But nothing was humorous about what had just happened.

Honestly, I just wanted to scream!

Literally nothing in my world made any sense these days.

Sonni was supposed to be playing dead but yet she was here and trying to meet up with Silas?

What the hell for?

Not me, her sister, but Silas.

A man that she'd only been around a handful of times…well at least to my knowledge.

There was no telling what the truth was behind this little situation, but I was going to make sure that whatever it was…came out.

Something in the water sure as hell wasn't clean and I was going to find out what was going on…

Again.

****

Chapter FIVE

"You're going out?" I asked Silas.

"Yes, just for a little while. Why?"

"Can you take Horizon with you?"

"Yeah. What's wrong? Are you okay?"

I nodded.

I was in recovery mode, but that wasn't going to stop me from snooping around while he was gone.

I'd just had an abortion the day before and physically and mentally, I wasn't feeling too good.

No, I didn't really want to have one.

I'd always been against them and vowed that I would never do something like that, but unfortunately I did.

I actually almost changed my mind seconds before.

I'd long since came had the birth control removed and I would have been super excited to find out that I was pregnant, but I wasn't.

There was no way to tell if the baby was Silas's or a product of the rape from Nolan.

Silas told me to keep it.

He was such a good guy.

He even said that if it wasn't his, he would've accepted it and took care of it anyway because the baby hadn't done anything wrong and it still would've deserved a father.

But I just couldn't do it.

I just couldn't look at my baby, every day, if it had been Nolan's, knowing how it was conceived.

It just wouldn't have been fair to the baby.

I just didn't think that I would have loved it the way that I was supposed to, even if I'd wanted to.

And there was the possibility of it being Silas's baby; which he wanted more than anything in the world, but there was just no way to be sure.

According to the doctor, I'd gotten pregnant on our "wedding-moon" and I just couldn't take any chances.

Hell we could always try again.

Depending on what I found when I went looking.

The abortion was what was best and with Silas and Horizon backing out of the driveway, the hunt was on!

Maybe Silas was too smart to stash anything important in the house but it was worth a look.

Sonni hadn't left my mind since the day that I'd saw her and if there was something to find, within my grasp, I was going to find it.

Instead of starting in the logical place, our bedroom, I decided to go to one of the bedrooms that we pretty much used as storage.

The house had a total of five bedrooms.

I hadn't had time to turn the empty ones into spares as of yet, so there was stuff all over the place in them.

I started to go through boxes and looking under the cushions of the abandoned sofa.

Every piece of paper I touched, I read, and ever bag, hole, or whatever, I made sure I stuck my hand in it.

Nothing.

Oh well, I was heading to the next empty bedroom.

I turned around…

"What the hell are you looking for Envy?" Silas asked.

I jumped.

He and Horizon were just standing there.

Neither of them had said a word.

I hadn't even heard the beeping noise that the door made to indicate that someone had come into the house.

My hand was on my chest as I tried to catch my breath.

Sneaky ass.

"I forgot my phone. And Horizon needed to go to the bathroom. Go ahead to the bathroom Horizon. So, what were you looking for Envy?" Silas asked again.

I didn't know how to answer him because hell I didn't really know what I was looking for.

I just knew that usually if you went looking, you were bound to find something.

I hadn't told him about the little meet-up with Sonni because not only had I not mentioned that I knew that she was still alive from our pre-honeymoon trip to the Bahamas, I didn't want him to go in "cover my tracks" mode, especially if he knew something in regards to dealings with Sonni.

I couldn't afford for him to shut down on me.

"Didn't I tell you that you could ask me anything and I would tell you?"

Silas said the statement as though he meant it.

Should I call his bluff?

Hell yeah!

"Sonni is alive. And she sent a letter to meet her at the park. I thought it was for me but it was for you. Why? Why does she want to meet with you? Did you know that she was still alive?"

"Yes. Sonni is blackmailing me Envy," Silas said.

What?

"At first I was paying her to keep quiet about knowing that I was the boss of the thirteenth floor. She didn't know about Grant; only me. I was paying her not to tell you. She'd spotted me one day in the office with Carmen, talking business, before you were even up there. She'd actually been standing by the door, listening to our entire conversation. Had she not been listening, she could have assumed that I was just a client, but because she listened, she knew that I was someone high up the chain, someone in charge. And then when you *introduced us*, so you thought, for the first time at the hospital, afterwards she popped up at your house one day with her request, and I'd been paying her to keep her mouth shut ever since. But later on, she confessed that she had something else. She said that she had proof of something that would put me away for a very long time. To this day, I don't even know what it is. But she said that she wasn't afraid to use it against me. I don't know if you know this, but your sister is a little crazy too. I mean like Carmen's kind of crazy," Silas said.

Duh!

So Sonni was blackmailing him?

For what?

What the hell did she have on him?

"No, she doesn't scare me. She said that she's made copies and that if anything ever happened to her, someone else had the information too and she'd told them what to do with it. I will admit, taking care of her *my* kind of way, usually would have been an option. She would have been "taken care of", but since she is your sister, I tried to take another route. But it hasn't been easy. And I'm just being honest with you. And I still have no idea what she knows. And then one day she came to me with her idea of wanting to get away and fake her death. I jumped at the idea because that meant that I no longer had to worry about her hanging anything over my head. Carmen is the one that put everything together to fake her death. I gave her one large pay out, the amount we agreed on, and overnight, she was gone. So, why she's back and wants to *meet*, your guess is as good as mine. We were never supposed to ever see or hear from her again. And all of that is the truth," Silas said.

I just looked at him and shook my head.

I could tell that he was telling the truth.

But the funny things was that I wished that he was lying.

When he'd told me that there were some things about him that I wouldn't need to know or that I would be much better off not knowing about, he was right.

What he'd just told me was one of those things.

I was disturbed and I didn't like the uneasy feeling that it gave me.

Silas looked at me for a moment longer and without another word, once Horizon returned from the bathroom, he grabbed her hand and seconds later, I heard the closing of the front door.

What?

So, Sonni has something that Silas didn't want to come out?

Whatever it was it had to be big!

And I was dying to know what it was.

I noticed that he hadn't went into details about any of the past shames, so I figured that whatever it was that she'd found had to be bad.

Or at least something that he knew for sure that he personally would go down for.

I didn't think that he was scared of what she knew. I just thought that whatever it was that she knew, he knew that it was going to have a major impact on his life.

And I had a feeling that it had something to do with me.

He hadn't tried to kill her or do anything bad to her because of his love for me, but he hadn't hesitated to help her disappear by choice.

Yeah, whatever it was had to be massive.

And Sonni knew the whole time that Silas was a *boss* and didn't say anything to me either?

That bitch!

How could she know that and not tell me?

I was her sister damn it!

I don't care if she didn't love me the way that she was supposed to or whatever, at some point, something in her had to tell her that what she was doing was a bit much.

Something in her had to tell her that I deserved to know.

All she had to do was open up her mouth and say something.

But no, she only wanted to use the information to get what she wanted.

She hadn't cared a thing about me or if I was possibly in harm's way.

She only cared about the money.

After all she'd done and said, I still loved her, but finding out this, I felt the closest thing to hate towards her for the very first time ever.

Screw her!

Sonni had said that friends helped her cover up her fake death, but really it had been Carmen.

I wondered if Carmen really didn't know that Sonni and I were sisters.

More than likely she probably did, despite what Sonni had said.

But that wasn't what was important.

I wanted to know what Sonni knew and if she ever planned on using it.

I was sure that Silas had paid her well, on top of whatever money she'd had from the hotel and wherever else, so something told me that it wasn't about the money anymore.

So what was it about?

Obviously whatever it was, it was from the past, so I was sure that I wouldn't hold it against him, at least I was going to try not to, but I was dying to know what it was and why he was so concerned that it could possibly destroy him.

So the question was, where in the hell was Sonni now?

Because this bitch, me, had a few questions!

***

"You mean the world to me," Silas said as we laid in the backyard, on a blanket, looking at the stars.

Horizon was in the house asleep and we were spending some much needed alone time together.

"I know."

Things had been so quiet and peaceful lately that things almost seemed normal.

We hadn't seen or heard from Carmen.

Sonni hadn't popped up again.

Silas and I had been getting along just fine.

Everything was good.

"Let's make a baby," Silas said.

I smiled at him.

I never imagined being with someone like him.

Whether I was referring to the good side of him or the bad side.

His good side was so damn good. Everything about him was perfect. Everything about him was what I needed and what I wanted in a man, in a husband, and in a father for my kids.

He was damn near perfect.

But on the flip side, the bad side, he was scary.

All of his power, the connections, the cover-ups, and Carmen were enough to make me want to run towards the nearest exit.

But for some reason I stayed.

For some reason I hadn't let go.

It had been long enough since the abortion and I figured that it was okay to start trying to put a bun in this oven again.

I might as well.

Making love to him under the stars, made me appreciate his love even more for some reason or another.

I just felt special.

I felt wanted.

I felt needed.

And to be honest, I felt complete.

I needed him just as much as he obviously needed me.

The cool air harassed my nipples as I rode Silas like the stallion that he was.

I closed my eyes and focused on enjoying the moment.

I could feel Silas's body stiffen beneath me, so I started to thrust my hips a tad bit harder so that I could *finish* with him.

After another minute or so, we released in unison and I smiled just before opening my eyes.

But...

"Ahh!" I screamed.

Carmen was standing there, only a few feet away from us.

"Eww," Carmen frowned.

What the hell was she doing in our backyard?

And she'd watched us have sex?

How sick!

"Silas, get off of your ass, and meet me out front. I need to talk to you. Envy, your tits are starting to sag. You should do something about that. Let me know if you need a doctor to help you out with a little *lift*," Carmen said and disappeared around the house.

I hate her!

I hated her so much that I wanted to cry.

Extremely bothered, I rolled off of Silas and he scurried to get dressed.

Why was she even here?

Again!

I'd told Silas to tell her not to come back to our house but obviously he hadn't relayed the message.

But I was about to.

I sat for just a few minutes to calm myself down and then I headed in the back door.

By the time I checked on Horizon, and made it to the living room to head for the front yard, the door opened and Silas came in.

I could tell that he was frustrated.

"What?" I questioned him.

Silas looked at me.

"Nothing."

I looked at him.

"I'm going to ask you one more time. What's going on and why did she come here?" I asked him, suddenly uninterested in hearing the bull crap, but felt the need to ask him anyway.

"I asked her to come by. She was supposed to come by earlier but never showed so I thought that she wasn't coming. I know you don't like her coming here, but here is the safest place for us to meet. I'm sure that she's still being watched, or at least her place probably is and we had a few loose ends to tie up. A few people to get paid. But it's all good now. It's all done," Silas said, lying the disk and folder that he was holding on the coffee table.

"That bitch better not come back to this house again. Or she can stay, and I'll go," I said behind Silas as he picked the things back up and headed to the bedroom.

***

"Envy, I thought that I could do it but I can't," my sister Josephine said.

I already knew what she was referring to.

Grant.

He couldn't do anything for himself, and Josephine was now pretty much a single mother and doing everything on her own, including taking care of him.

I told her to hire some help for both the kids and with Grant, but she hadn't listened.

"Well, what are you going to do? The doctors said that he will never get better so are you going to stick by him like you said that you would? Or stick him in some kind of facility?"

I waited for Josephine to respond.

"No silly, I'm going to kill him," she said.

What?

Maybe I hadn't heard her right.

"Kill him?"

"Yes. I could never live with myself if I placed him in some kind of facility. You never know what those folks would do to him. They would never take care of him the way that I have. My only option is to kill him. I'm sure that he would rather be dead anyway."

Wait a minute…huh?

What the hell was Josephine talking about?

How could she even think something like that?

Shaking my head, I focused back on my conversation with Josephine.

"Don't kill him. I'll find somewhere to put him that's nice and Silas and I will pay for it," I said.

"Did you forget that we are rich too? I don't need your money or your help Envy. I already told you what I was going to do," Josephine said and changed the subject.

If Silas ever found out that she'd told me about this beforehand, he would surely kill me for not saying anything.

I knew that I was going to have to tell him.

We talked for a few minutes more and I called Silas right after.

"Hey, where are you?" I asked him.

Silas had been on the go lately.

I figured that he probably was still meeting up with Carmen but since she couldn't come to the house, he was probably sneaking off to meet her somewhere.

Then again, he said that everything had been handled, so maybe he was doing other things.

I personally needed to find me a few things to do.

Since I no longer "worked" at the hotel, I was home all the time.

I had nothing to do all day besides tend to Horizon and soon she would be starting school.

And I couldn't believe it.

My baby was growing up on me.

So, soon, she would be gone all day and I really would be bored out of my mind.

I really needed to find some friends.

I'd asked Silas about the wives of all of the friends that he'd introduced me to, but he'd had to tell me the truth.

He'd paid all of them to pretend to be his friends.

They all were either connections, or in his circle for whatever reason, but he'd paid them to show up and pretend whenever the occasion caused for it.

The audacity!

The stupid things that people do when they had money.

I'd actually laughed aloud when he told me because it was just so stupid.

He'd gone through all of that and for what?

To impress me?

Hell, I didn't have friends either so I wouldn't have had anything to say about his lack thereof.

So basically, Grant was his only real friend.

But, I was worried about me at the moment and this sista' needed friends and I needed to find a hobby.

"I'm on my way home. What's up?"

"Oh nothing, I'll just talk to you when you get here," I said to him and once we hung up, I decided to go outside for some fresh air.

The Fall wasn't too far away and with that being my favorite time of the year; I couldn't wait for the leaves to paint the streets with orange and brown leaves and for the Fall weather to remind me that the holidays were on their way again.

I looked around the neighborhood at the other house and tried to guess the life that they had behind closed doors.

I wondered if they were happy or if they had just as much crazy drama in their lives as I did.

Happiness seemed to be one of the most expensive things in the world these days, and I hated the moments that I'd always taken for granted.

I remembered a time in my early teenage years.

Before I'd even started dating Keymar.

I remembered being so full of ideas, and I had so many goals and dreams.

There were so many things that I was going to do.

I had my life all figured out. I had a plan. But nothing that I'd planned had come true.

I hadn't accomplished one single goal.

But all of that was about to change.

My husband had more than enough money, and so did I, somewhere, so it was time to make some of my dreams a reality.

It was time to make my dreams come true.

Silas pulled up and I greeted him with a smile.

I approached him and without hesitating, I told him of Josephine's issues with Grant and suggested that he do something about it.

I didn't tell him that Josephine wanted to kill him, but I did express that I thought that she might be overwhelmed.

Silas understood and come the next day, the situation was handled.

Josephine called cursing and fussing stating that Silas and Grant's parents had come to take Grant away and that Silas even came with papers for her to sign for a legal divorce.

She said that he told her to move on with her life, and that she didn't have to worry about Grant anymore.

She'd said that he suggested that she never try to see him or contact his parents again.

To me that was a little harsh being that there were kids involved, but hell anything was better than her trying to kill him.

She said Silas made sure that she had access to all of Grant's money, since he wouldn't need it anyway, and then she said he invited her and the kids over to our house for Sunday dinner.

I listened to Josephine as she became emotional, but I knew that she was going to be okay.

The way that I saw it was that she'd tried and was willing to make the best of her marriage, but it just hadn't been in the plan.

So now she was free.

She was free to live and get back some of the time that she'd lost due to marrying so young and becoming a mother.

I actually offered her to go into business with me as soon as I figured out what it was that I wanted to do or open.

I definitely had a feeling that everything was finally going to be okay.

But knowing my life…I was wrong.

***

I woke up with a tray of food on Silas's side of the bed.

He'd said that he had gone to the grocery store and to run a few errands and that I should be dressed by the time that he got back so that we could go to an early movie and then do a little shopping.

Horizon was going to kindergarten, so we had to get a few things.

She was getting so big and it wouldn't be long before she was a teenager and then heading off to college.

The adoption was official and her last name had been changed to match mine and Silas's.

We seemed like one big happy family.

I just hoped that we could actually get to that place.

Things were good but there were always concerns.

I wondered if relocating, out of state would make things better, but no matter how far we ran, our problems would find us.

Hell, we moved an hour away from the city and people were still finding out where we lived and popping up unannounced.

I ate the breakfast that Silas had prepared for me and then I headed to shower.

I hadn't really dressed up and a while, so I felt like looking expensive.

I dressed in a red romper with gold Gucci flats, just because I wasn't in the mood for heels. All gold accessories, a gold flower in my hair and even my make-up consisted of golds and a popping red lipstick.

I headed to the living room to sit for a while and to wait around for them to arrive.

I tried watching TV but that didn't work. I tried playing a game on my phone, but that didn't work either.

So, I figured maybe I would go outside and catch a breeze.

I've always loved the outdoors.

And with all of the trees and the ceiling fans on the front porch, it was never too bad relaxing outside, no matter what the temperature was for the day.

Flipping on the porch ceiling fans, I opened the front door and I was shocked to find Sonni standing there.

She was holding a decorated box.

So she was the one who had left the box full of pictures on Valentine's Day?

Why?

It must have something to do with this whole blackmailing Silas thing.

I could tell that she didn't expect me to catch her but I was glad that I did.

She owed me a few explanations.

"Sonni," I said and at the sound of her name, she dropped the box and turned around and started to run.

And you know what, I started running after her.

Well, it was kind of like a fast walk, but whatever you wanted to call it.

"Sonni wait," I called behind her but she just kept running.

By the time she neared the end of the driveway, I paused and figured that I would never be able to catch her.

"Sonni, I know that you are blackmailing Silas. I just want to know why. Why!" I screamed behind her.

At the sound of that, Sonni looked back at me but...

She didn't stop running.

A car came out of nowhere and before I could open my mouth to warn her, the red car slammed right into her and I watched her body fly towards the windshield, roll down the hood and then hit the ground.

Did that just happen?

And why couldn't I move?

Why were my feet frozen in place?

I watched the car back away, and drive away as though they hadn't done anything at all.

My mouth opened but still I didn't run to her aid.

And I wasn't going to.

Before, I couldn't understand how Carmen had done nothing to help her sister and her niece the day of their deaths but at that moment, it seemed like the best thing for me to do.

For me, and my husband.

She hated me, unintentionally, and because of how she was and her selfishness, I wasn't far from hating her.

I didn't want to feel that way, but I did.

And she was trying to ruin my husband's life.

But we were just getting in a good place and I didn't want things to change.

Maybe this was for the best.

Maybe it was time to choose me.

Mind made up, as neighbors came out to help Sonni, I turned my back to her and went back into the house.

After all, she was supposed to be dead a long time ago anyway.

****

Chapter SIX

I stared at Carmen and Detective Wiley.

I was confused by what I was seeing.

They were smiling, laughing and holding hands.

Huh?

Last I checked, he hated Carmen and he wanted nothing more in the whole world than to see her rot in prison for what she'd done to his best friend, because she was the cause of his suicide.

But there they were, right in front of me, laughing, smiling at each other, about to pay for their food.

I'd decided to come to the mall, and I'd spotted them in the food court before I'd even had a chance to get started with some shopping.

At first I was going to keep walking, but something strange was definitely going on around here, and I wasn't faking the funk for anyone, anymore.

They paid for their food and turned around to see me standing there.

Both of them looked as though they were constipated and they didn't even try to hide their discomfort.

"What an unpleasant surprise," I said.

Both of them just stared at me.

But that didn't stop me from talking.

"Detective Wiley, I thought you hated her?" I questioned him.

Carmen looked at him.

"I did, but," he started to say.

"But what?" I cut him off.

"None of your damn business," Carmen said.

"You're right. It isn't. You guys can die together for all I care. And I can enjoy the rest of my life with my husband. Boy, wait until I tell him this," I said with a smile.

But the look on Carmen's face had gone from defensive to terrified, in only a matter of seconds.

Hmm…

"No, you can't tell Silas," Carmen said.

What?

What was she talking about?

Why couldn't I tell Silas?

What did he have to do with what was going on with her and the detective?

"And why the hell not?" I asked her.

She and Detective Wiley looked at each other.

"Look. You just can't. If you don't tell him, you will never have to worry about me again. I swear to you that I will never come around or bother you and your family again. I won't call or talk to Silas, at all. You have my word."

What?

For Carmen to make such a huge deal, or promise, it must be serious.

Whatever the reason behind it all had to be damn serious for her to agree to never speak to Silas again.

And you know what, more than I wanted to know what the reason was...I wanted her out of our lives even more.

I wanted a fair chance at happiness with Silas, and a life without Carmen would definitely guarantee that.

"Deal. But if you ever call him, come by my house, or if he so much as mention that he spoke to you, I'm telling," I said and once she nodded, I walked away.

Wow.

Now that was weird.

To see the two of them, together, just didn't make sense.

I mean, the whole hotel bust and putting me through hell to bring her down, was all for nothing basically.

I just didn't understand it.

And furthermore, if they were an item…eww!

Carmen was *sick*, physically, so did that mean that he was sick too?

I was so confused, but at this point, it didn't even matter.

Carmen was out of our lives for good.

Silas and I might have a chance at this thing after all. Carmen was gone.

Sonni was gone.

Sonni died, for real this time, that day in the street.

A few others had seen the hit and run as well, and someone had told the police that I was outside during that accident.

But when they questioned me I told them that I was going to check the mail and that I had no idea who she was or why she had been running in the first place.

They'd found a car that had belonged to her a little ways up the street from my house and due to her fake identity information, she was identified as Savannah.

So now, *they* were both dead.

Silas had arrived home to get me that day just as they were cleaning up and I told him what happened.

Unfortunately I had forgotten to pick up the box from the front porch, and Silas took it without letting me see what was inside.

At first I made a big deal about it, but he pointed out that whatever was inside was pointless.

He set the box on fire right in front of me.

So, whatever it was, it was gone.

And so was she.

I guess now we would never know her reason for coming back.

But at least we knew that she had been up to no good.

I tried to feel bad about it all, but I didn't.

I'd just become so unattached somehow after the realization that she'd been telling the truth the whole time, when she would say that she didn't give a damn about anyone but herself.

And her words to me at the park that day and then finding out what she knew from Silas, was just the icing on the cake.

I guess it kind of really was hate that I felt for her.

I did make sure that she was buried though.

It was the least that I could do.

After no one had claimed her for a few days, Silas had some stings pulled and had someone fake to be her sister and identify her body.

I wasn't proud of the way that I'd handled things or the way that I felt but at the time, it's just how it was.

Maybe this feeling would eventually pass and I knew that probably down the line it would hit me like a tidal wave and I would probably never be able to forgive myself for my actions.

Maybe one day, I could go pay my respects to her, genuinely.

But I didn't see that happening anytime soon.

After all, it's not like I was the one that killed her.

I was just trying to talk to her.

She was the one running away from me as though I was going to attack her.

She acted as though she couldn't even give me a decent conversation.

So it wasn't my fault.

It was hers.

They still hadn't been able to find the car or the driver but according to the news, they were looking for them.

The news only had the picture from Sonni's fake license as Savannah, and in my opinion, it didn't really look like her.

I mean it was her, but maybe she'd intentionally taken such a horrible picture.

Anyway, when they showed her on the news, I'd waited to see if Josephine or any estranged family reached out to ask or talk about the similarities that the "dead woman" had with Sonni, but no one ever called.

So, nothing was said and there were no worries.

Taking a deep breath, I entered the first store, ready for some so much needed retail therapy.

I dismissed all thoughts of Carmen and Sonni and I realized that my happily ever after might not be too far away.

That's if Carmen actually kept her word.

***

"Silas where is Nolan?" I asked him hesitantly.

"Do you really want to know?"

Did I?

I guess I did.

"He's in prison in Mexico. For the next 40 years, but I doubt that he will make it even a year. Last I checked he wasn't doing so well. Seems that the inmates have a way of making rapists pay for their crimes in their own special way," Silas said.

I didn't say anything.

I could only imagine how bad prison was in Mexico.

No, I didn't feel sorry for him at this point, but did Silas really have to have him locked up all the way down there?

So what, did he know the prison warden or something?

There was no telling.

I couldn't even begin to imagine how Silas had pulled something like that off and I wasn't about to ask him.

A thing like this was why his power scared the crap out of me.

Next time I'll just keep my questions to myself.

But at least he hadn't killed him.

"Can I ask you a question Envy?" Silas asked.

I shook my head yes.

"When were you going to tell me that you were pregnant again?" Silas smiled.

I smiled back.

Silas was assuming but he was on to something.

I hadn't had a period in over two months now.

I'd been so consumed with other things and opening my boutique that I hadn't really paid much attention to it.

"I made you a doctor's appointment for tomorrow," he smiled and started to kiss my stomach.

I giggled.

"I could've made my own appointment. Stop using your power or whatever you want to call it and just be a regular husband," I said to him.

"That's what I want more than anything in the world. To just be regular," Silas replied and I could tell that he was serious.

"Would you love me if I didn't have money and power? Would you still want me? Would you still want to be with me if I was just a regular man, with a regular job and regular money?"

I nodded.

"Yes I would. Having money and all of these nice things, isn't what I thought that it would be. I almost wish I could just go back to being broke at times. Before I had gone to the thirteenth floor. Life wasn't easy. But in a way it was a lot better," I said.

"Well let's give it up. Let's give it all up. Take just enough and give all of this up and let this life go. Let's be regular, together. We can go somewhere, anywhere. Take enough money to get settled. I'll become a regular man and find a regular job. We can become the perfect, little, regular family," Silas said.

I looked at him.

Was he serious?

"Are you serious?" I asked him.

"Yes. Dead serious."

I was shocked that he said it and though I wanted to say yes, I really did, but I knew that we couldn't; at least not at the moment.

The store was still in the process of getting built and not to mention that we might have a baby on the way.

Now might not be the best time.

"Maybe we could---," I started to say but Silas cut me off.

"Never mind Envy," he said with an attitude.

What?

What did I say wrong?

He's the one that mentioned the whole *maybe baby* thing, and then turned around and asked if we could go back to being broke.

We could.

Just after the store was finished and if I wasn't pregnant.

Then we could do whatever he wanted to do.

But Silas headed to the kitchen in a sudden bad mood, and I headed to the bedroom to get the extra pregnancy test that I had stashed away.

Waiting for the results to pop up took forever!

Finally the two lines showed up and confirmed that I was indeed pregnant.

I smiled and ran out of the bathroom to see that Silas was now sitting on the bed.

Before I could say anything, he spoke.

"Told you," was all he said.

***

Time was flying and I cried as I dropped Horizon off at school for the first day.

I knew that this day would come, and I'd tried to prepare for it, but I was an emotional wreck.

She was getting so big, so fast.

And to think that I was about to do it all over again.

I was around eleven weeks pregnant and I didn't like it one bit.

Since I'd had the abortion so fast, I'd barely experienced any symptoms, but this pregnancy definitely had me feeling all kinds of ways.

I was sick.

I was emotional.

I was sick.

I was hungry.

I was sick.

I was horny.

And did I mention that I was sick?

It was really that bad.

And I hated it!

I hated everything about it and I couldn't wait for it all to be over.

But Silas was enjoying every minute of it.

He was so loving and attentive and I couldn't have asked for a better husband and father for my child.

He was always there and he tried to do anything that he could to make sure that I was comfortable and to make sure that I was okay.

He was amazing!

But the pregnancy…oh, it was of the devil!

I drove away from the charter school, still in tears, and decided that I would stop and get breakfast.

Silas was at home asleep, and was going to be bummed that I didn't wake him so that he could see Horizon off on her first day of school, but I'd ran him around so much the day before, that I knew that he was tired.

And I decided to let him get his rest.

Hopefully he would forgive me if I came back with breakfast.

Finally making up my mind as to where I wanted to go, I parked in the last parking space on the curb and prepared to get out.

Unable to reach my purse on the floor on the passenger's side, I opened the door to give me a little more room to stretch for it.

I grabbed my purse and just as I was about to get out I noticed that my wallet had fallen out of it and had been laying under it so I leaned back over to get it and…

It happened so fast that it was almost a blur, but looking at the driver's side door lying in the middle of the street, my vision became extremely clear.

At the screeching of tires, I glanced at the red Charger as it turned the corner.

Say it aint so!

Was that the same car that had hit Sonni?

Huh?

I stared at the door as I sat back in my seat.

They'd knocked the door clean off of my Toyota.

I'd chosen to drive it instead of the Escalade, since it hadn't been driven in so long, and I figured that it was time to take it for a spin.

Had I have gotten out of the car with my purse, without catching sight of my wallet on the floor, I would have been lying in the street right beside of the banged up door.

Someone had just tried to kill me.

This was no accident and remembering the speeding red Charger with the dark tinted windows.

It sure as hell looked like the same car that had hit Sonni, so, that meant that whoever had killed her, was trying to kill me.

But who?

Why?

Who in the hell wanted me dead?

This wasn't my first brush with death.

But this time, and maybe because I was pregnant, or because I'd identified that it might have been the same person that had killed my sister, I felt as though my heart had been broken.

A weird way of feeling, but that's how bad my heart started to ache.

I started to cry uncontrollably as people rushed over to make sure that I was okay.

I couldn't speak.

I couldn't do anything.

They asked for my phone to contact a family member, and I unlocked it and pressed Silas's number.

Some random man tried to explain to Silas what had happened, but after only a few seconds, he was talking to himself.

Silas must have hung up.

Well of course he was on his way.

I heard the sirens and through my tears, I saw the lights.

As far as I knew, physically, I was fine.

I couldn't have been more thankfully for being too lazy to get out of the car to walk around to the other side.

I was supposed to be dead.

I was supposed to be gone.

While I was being checked out in the back of the ambulance, there was a knock at the door.

I just knew that it was Silas, but I was wrong.

It was Detective Wiley.

I was surprised to see him at first, but then I had to remember that he was an officer, if he could still be called that considering his title.

"Envy are you okay?"

I looked at him.

His voice was different.

He didn't seem so rude or arrogant.

His face was less tensed and he just didn't seem like the same man.

Oh no, he was a man in love.

And with Carmen?

Eww!

"What happened Envy?"

I told him everything that I knew.

I even told him that the car was the same one that was described on the news for the hit and run a little while ago.

I didn't mention that the hit and run involved my sister, but who was to say that he didn't already know that.

He was with Carmen now, so he couldn't be trusted. Period.

And there was no telling what Carmen knew or if she was up to something but I couldn't worry about that at the moment.

I was just concerned about my life and the life of my unborn child.

And where the hell was Silas!

"Well let me know if there is anything that I can do," Detective Wiley said and he went on his merry little way.

A minute or two later, I finally saw him.

My Silas.

"Baby are you okay? Are you hurt? How is the baby? Is the baby okay?" Silas asked a thousand questions all at once and all I could do was cry and shake my head.

He joined me in the back of the ambulance and hugged and kissed me.

He wasn't crying but I could surely tell that he wanted to.

I wasn't sure if it was because he was emotional or frightened.

Or if it was because he was angry.

I could see so many things in him all at the same time, and I thought that he was going to explode.

But he kept his cool.

Of course they wanted to take me to the hospital, just to make sure and to check on the baby, so the workers asked Silas if he was going with me and at his answer, they closed the door and pulled off.

I was still crying but my mind was all over the place.

Now that I knew that whoever was responsible for hitting and killing Sonni, was now out to kill me too, the sympathy and remorse that I hadn't felt for my sister, was starting to kick in.

Someone had killed her on purpose.

It wasn't an accident.

They had to have known that she was there, at that exact time, and they took that opportunity as soon as it presented itself.

She'd been murdered.

Someone had murdered my sister and now they were out to get me too

But who?

Whoever it was had to have a reason. Whoever it was obviously had something against Sonni and me, but I couldn't imagine who it could be.

But whoever it was also knew where I lived and now my home was no longer safe.

Nolan was in prison.

It couldn't be him.

Carmen seemed to be happy in a new relationship.

So why would it be her?

Silas and I were on the best of terms.

So who?

Who wanted to kill me?

Who'd want to kill me *and* Sonni for that matter?

It just didn't make sense.

Silas called Josephine to tell her what happened and she asked to speak to me, but I didn't feel like talking.

I just wanted to know what was going on.

My life was in such a good place, for all of two seconds, and then here comes something else.

I just needed a freaking break!

When was all of this going to end?

When could I have a normal life, be a normal mother, and have a normal marriage?

When damn it, when!

I told Silas my thoughts and that it was the same car that had hit Sonni, or at least it looked identical to it if it wasn't.

The more I talked about it, it was as though a light bulb went off or something because I started to think about something.

I started to search my thoughts.

I tried to remember every word.

I had been in complete shock at the beginning, but I was almost positive about something.

I looked at Silas who was now doing something on his phone.

I wasn't sure if the question that I was about to ask him was going to cause a problem, but I just had to ask.

"Silas?"

He looked at me concerned.

"How did you know where I was?" I asked him.

"What?"

"How did you know where I was? I didn't hear the man on the phone tell you where I was. He told you what happened, but he didn't tell you where I was. How did you know?" I asked him suspiciously.

I replayed the conversation over and over and I was positive that Silas had hung up before the stranger had disclosed the location.

He'd told Silas what had happened to me but he hadn't told him where I was.

So how in the hell had Silas known where to come to?

"I headed towards Horizon's school and figured that I was bound to run into you and the accident along the way. I hung up out of anger and by the time I realized that I didn't know where I was going, I called your phone over and over but no answer. So I just drove until I came up on the scene. I knew it had to be somewhere along the way. I was actually on the phone with a connection at the police station, just in case I couldn't find it. He was looking into it, but I found you before he was able to tell me anything."

I listened to Silas and found my purse that the police had placed in the ambulance with me.

"Check it," Silas said.

I guess he knew that I just had to be sure.

Our history and pasts, told me that I always had to check…twice.

I found my phone and saw that Silas had called more times than I could even count.

I let out a deep breath.

He was telling the truth.

Silas stared at me.

I couldn't exactly make out what he was thinking or what was on his mind, but when he touched my stomach, I figured that maybe his thoughts were on something else and not so much as the trust issues concerning me.

I laid my head on his shoulder and allowed a few more tears to flow.

"Who did this to me Silas? Who wants me dead?"

Silas took a long, sorrowful, deep breath.

"I don't know. But on my life, I'm going to find out."

****

Chapter SEVEN

"It's a boy!"

The smile on Silas's face was priceless.

I'd never seen him so happy.

The twinkle in his eyes reminded me of the last firework of a light show.

You know the big bad ass one. The big finale; the one that everyone waited for and the reason that everyone stuck around to the end just to see it.

That's the look that was in Silas's eyes, and to be totally honest, I was happy that I had contributed to making him so happy.

He was going to have a son.

What man didn't want a son?

The rest of the doctor's visit went well and we pretty much skipped out of the place hand and hand.

We decided to go look at a few things since we finally knew the sex of the baby.

Maybe it was too soon, but we didn't care about that.

Our little prince was going to have the world.

We headed into a store and darn near went crazy.

We were picking out all kinds of things for the baby.

We were so happy despite everything that had happened.

Of course no one knew who was behind the hits and runs as of yet, but Silas was pulling every string he had to track them down.

But so far, no luck.

But we tried not to talk or think about it.

We'd moved out of the house so that I could feel safe.

We hadn't sold it, nor had we done anything with it yet.

All of our stuff was still there and everything, except for clothes and things like that that we'd brought with us.

For the time being we were living in a condo that of course Silas mysteriously up and said that he owned but had failed to mention it.

He later had to explain that he owned all kinds of things; including portions of sports teams and things of that nature.

I told him that one day we were definitely going to have to have one long ass conversation where we laid every single thing that we'd ever done, been tied to, been connected with or whatever, out on the table.

Silas agreed.

We walked around the store and just as we turned the corner to check out strollers, my mouth dropped open.

It was Carmen.

And she was pregnant.

Carmen was pregnant?

Um, okay.

She saw us and immediately turned her back to us, but oh no, she wasn't getting off that easy.

Maybe she was trying to stick to her word in regards to Silas, but screw that, I wanted to be nosey.

"Carmen, you're pregnant?"

She turned around.

Silas spoke to her but she didn't speak back.

Wow.

So, she was serious about keeping away.

Silas hadn't mentioned her lately and every time I said something about her he said that he hadn't heard from or spoken to her.

He never seemed disappointed or concerned, so I figured that maybe she really hadn't reached out to him, and maybe he didn't really even care.

Looking at Carmen's belly, she looked to be around the same amount of months as I was.

She hadn't said anything so I asked her another question.

"How far along are you?"

She just looked at me.

"She asked you a question," Silas chimed and guess what, at the sound of his voice, the bitch spoke.

"I'm four months."

What the hell!

What, so Silas had some kind of mind control over her or something?

"What are you having?"

"A boy," Carmen said and before I could open my mouth to say another word, she left her cart full of clothes and headed out of the store.

Well, that was weird.

And who in the hell would get her pregnant?

I couldn't help but wonder if it was Detective Wiley's baby, and of course her health status crossed my mind.

Detective Wiley knew what was going on with Carmen and her health, so I found it weird that he would actually even go there, and get on that level with Carmen.

Not to mention that she had been with his friend and was the cause of his suicide.

Definitely a weird scenario.

I looked at Silas who was minding his own business, but I was definitely about to get all up in it.

"That baby ain't yours is it?"

Silas looked at me as though he wanted to knock my head clean off of my shoulders.

"What kind of stupid ass question is that Envy huh? Stupid ass," Silas bellowed and threw his wallet at me, just before he walked out the store.

What the hell just happened?

It was just a damn question.

And who in the hell was he talking to like that?

Embarrassed that the other pregnant ladies had seen Silas overact, I paid for the things that I currently had and headed out the door.

When Silas saw me, he got out of the car and took the bags from my hands.

He didn't say anything and didn't bother to give me any kind of eye contact.

So, he was really pissed off.

He was big mad huh?

But why though?

It wasn't that big of a deal, especially if he didn't have anything to do with Carmen's pregnancy.

Or did he?

"I'm sorry. I was just asking."

"Asking for what Envy? I don't want Carmen. Why would you even ask me something like that? No, she is definitely not pregnant by me Envy if that's what you wanted to hear," Silas screamed.

He was really upset.

That's all he had to say in the first place.

Wait a minute…was he jealous?

Was he feeling some kind of way because Carmen was pregnant?

I dared not ask him, but his behavior was definitely out of the normal and a little suspect.

We rode in silence the rest of the way home.

Hmm…

***

Christmas had come and gone, and I was spending time with Josephine before she said goodbye.

She had been so distant lately and I hadn't really spoken to her much, but once I did, I wasn't happy.

Though I was totally against it, and though I felt that the kids were going to be so confused, Josephine was moving away…to live near, with, or whatever, Sonni's previous husband Mark.

She said that it had nothing to do with them and that it had everything to do with the kids.

She said her kids needed a father figure and Sonni's kids needed a mother.

So she was taking the money, and running to him.

To be honest, I felt as though she just wanted to get away.

She just wanted a new beginning and I could definitely understand that.

She said that her and Mark weren't going to have anything more than some weird ass co-parenting relationship.

After all, some of her kids were probably his anyway.

"Why don't you and Silas pick up and move too. I mean life on the west coast is probably completely different and since you've been through quite a bit here, lately, why not? Just pick up and go. That's what I'm doing. I'm just going to go. There's no telling what's in store for me there but I'm going to find out," Josephine said as she took a sip of her tea.

I couldn't believe that she'd had a change of heart, but I guess what went on with her destruction of a wedding and what happened to Grant had pushed her there.

Silas or Josephine never even mentioned Grant these days.

Josephine never said one word about him and since Silas had taken him somewhere safe, he'd made it clear that he didn't want to be reminded of what had happened to his best friend.

But I hated that it had happened that way.

And now my sister was moving away from me.

"Don't go," I said to her.

She helped me with Horizon and I was about to have a son.

I needed her there with me.

I didn't have any friends.

I just had her and Silas.

"I have to go. Being in my house, and in this state, just reminds me of so many things, that I just want to forget. Talk to Silas. Maybe one day you guys will be ready for a change and join us," Josephine said as she hugged me.

I wanted to cry but I didn't.

It wasn't fair.

Maybe I could talk Silas into moving away.

Hell, I was afraid to live in our house and I felt the same way that Josephine did about all of the things that had happened in the last few years.

Moving away just might be the cure.

But with Horizon being in her first year, I would have to let her finish out the school year.

I just couldn't pull her out just like that.

She was still getting used to the process.

But summer was a few months away and the baby would be born and a few months by then, so maybe moving then was really something to consider.

Josephine talked for a few more minutes and then she was gone, and I was left to try to sort out my feelings.

Silas and Horizon were watching a movie in the bedroom, so I decided to take a bubble bath.

I was as big as a whale and standing up to shower just wasn't an option these days.

Besides, I wanted to sit, relax, and think about my life and family.

Josephine and I had actually gone to visit our parents, as well as my sister Tia's and my nephew's, graves the other day.

She'd wanted to tell them that she wouldn't be back to visit them for a while.

I'd just gone along because I really did miss them.

If they were all here, I couldn't imagine how good life would have been.

My life would have definitely turned out a lot different.

Nolan and Grant briefly crossed my mind.

Grant's situation was unfortunate, and even though Nolan had done something so horrible to me, I couldn't help but think about whether or not he was still alive.

But I was sure that I would never know.

I'd brought my phone into the bathroom so that I could listen to the music saved to it, but just as I started to select a song, it started to ring.

Carmen.

Of course I still had her number.

And apparently she still had mine.

"What?"

"Can we talk? I need your help."

What?

She needed *my* help?

Now I just had to hear this!

"Help for what Carmen?"

"Don't say my name. Is Silas around you?"

Carmen actually sounded frightened, which threw me for a loop.

Could she really be in trouble?

Did she really need my help?

Did I really even care?

Ugh, I knew better than to get involved, and I definitely knew not to trust Carmen, but something in me told me that she knew some things that I needed to know.

So, I got out of the tub, and told Silas that I was going for a ride.

He questioned me, but I convinced him that Josephine leaving was heavy on my mind and that I just needed to ride and clear my head.

Finally, he understood.

I met Carmen at the same baby store that we'd seen each other last.

I figured that we would blend in and no one would be paying us much attention.

Carmen was already there when I walked in.

I approached her cautiously.

She was a lot bigger than I was and I was big!

She looked like she was about to pop.

"Silas is trying to kill me."

What?

No greeting, no hey, no small talk or nothing.

Same ole' Carmen.

But what did she mean that Silas was trying to kill her?

"How do you know that?"

Carmen looked at me strange.

"The only one who doesn't really know Silas is you. I know him. And I know that he is trying to kill me."

Carmen's mouth was just so *fly* and the way that my hormones were set up these days, she didn't want it.

She really didn't want *it*.

"Why would he want to kill you Carmen?"

"Hell, why did he want to kill you?"

What?

What the hell was she talking about?

Silas wanted to kill me?

When?

Why?

"So, Silas tried to or wanted to kill me?"

"No."

"Then why did you say it?"

Carmen was looking around the store like a crazy person. She was definitely watching her surroundings.

"Look. This is about me. Not you. He doesn't want to kill you now so that's all you need to worry about. He loves you. He wouldn't hurt you. But he is trying to kill me," Carmen spit out.

My mind was still trying to figure out why Silas would have wanted to kill me in the first place.

What had I done to him?

"Why Carmen? Why does he want to kill you?"

She looked at me.

"Because I'm pregnant by his brother."

What?

What brother?

Huh?

"Silas has a brother? Here? In the states?"

"Yes. Silas's real dad was American. His mother had an affair on her husband with an American man while she was here in the states. She was frowned upon, and even forbidden to ever contact him or return to America, but she was permitted to still have the child. Sure she told Silas the truth and once he came to the states, he searched for him, his real dad, but he had long passed away. But he did find a few siblings. Wiley, or Detective Wiley as you call him, is one of them. His half-brother on his father's side."

What in the world!

It just didn't make any sense.

How in the hell...

Why in the hell...

What the hell!

Silas had siblings?

Detective Wiley was his brother?

I was so confused.

"I'm about to tell you something. The whole operation from the hotel was a set up. A plan for us all to get out without the investors, clients and sponsors knowing; without Silas's family and the family that actually owned the hotel knowing. All tracks had to be covered from the original owners of the hotel and organizers of the thirteenth floor, and Silas's family. So we came up with the perfect plan. Especially since no one knows about Silas and Wiley being brothers, it all worked out fine. Wiley really is a detective and so he had to follow protocol, build up the case, cause awareness, and of course, get you to follow the steps as though you were really doing something. It was all a part of the plan Envy. We all wanted out. Of course Silas wouldn't dare see you behind bars, so you were to be used as the witness in return granted freedom because all of the other people have really faced criminal charges."

Wait a minute now.

That damn Silas was something else I tell you.

Well, he tried to tell you partial truths, but not the whole truth, so it was still a lie in my eyes.

And he and the detective were brothers?

And the whole thing was set up?

Unbelievable!

"We were all just so tired of it. Silas, Grant and myself. Wiley was just brought in and paid handsomely to make everything look legit and flow smoothly. He faced bad financial troubles after his divorce. His wife was the one who had made the big bucks."

Pregnancy getting the best of us, we made our way to some chairs and took a seat.

"I just would have never thought…I mean, I just don't understand."

"When is the last time that you got paid for thinking? You don't get paid for thinking Envy. And you don't have to understand it but the truth is the truth."

"So you're not sick? You don't have HIV? And you didn't sleep with Detective Wiley's friend and make him commit suicide?"

Carmen shook her head.

"Hell no. I'm just fine. Wiley went overboard with that whole story. Actually, his wife left him for his best friend. And then she left his best friend for his cousin; whom she had been sleeping with the whole time, and had given him HIV. And then he committed suicide. Talk about karma. I guess Wiley was just caught up in pretending. He lied. I'm assuming you might have asked or mentioned something that made him feel the need to go off the deep in with that whole story. He'd had to call Silas and inform him of the story, about me, so that Silas wasn't caught off guard if you asked him or mentioned. It was all made up; the parts about me anyway. You're not supposed to know any of this. But I don't know what else to do. The only weakness that Silas has is you," Carmen said.

I was flabbergasted.

These people were absolutely crazy!

They lied about every damn thing!

I was known to tell a little lie, here or there, but these folks had me beat.

Carmen didn't even have HIV!

What!

Detective Wiley had been playing along the whole time.

Wow!

And oh Silas, well, I just wasn't going to even go there at the moment.

"Wiley is my son's father. And Silas found out. You see, Silas doesn't love me, but he's so used to me loving him that he's uses it. He uses it to have control over me. He knows that I have always done anything that he says. Even after he done what he did to me, I couldn't quite stop loving him, in my own, crazy little way that is. My love is a little different, which was always the problem, but still, he knew that whatever it was that had a stronghold on me, he could use it to control me."

Interesting.

And I was pissed to maximum capacity, but I didn't show it.

"Wiley and I were a mistake. It was a night that wasn't supposed to happen, but once it did, it never stopped and I came up pregnant. Really, I was just doing it to do it. No feelings attached. I hadn't spoken a word about it to Silas and I'd told him that I was going to let him get on with his life and move on, but neither Wiley nor I told him about us. We just weren't going to say anything. That's why I needed you not to tell him that you saw us being so *friendly*. Anyway, after he saw me here that day, pregnant, he came by. He wanted to know who the father was but I wouldn't tell him. Being told *no* by me didn't sit well with him. But I'd known that he would find a way to find out and he did. And he made sure that I knew that he knew. And I have been having strange things happen to me ever since. He's trying to kill me. I know he is. And I need your help to stop him," Carmen said.

I didn't know what to say.

My mind was on overload and I needed a drink.

Pregnant and all.

I needed a damn drink!

I just didn't know what to say or what to believe anymore.

The lies and the secrets surrounding the people in my life were just too much.

Carmen went on to say that she was the one that had me shot at her house that day.

I knew that bitch had something to do with it!

She admitted that she was in a bad place and that she'd told Detective Wiley to shot me but not kill me.

Just for her entertainment.

Just because Silas loved me and not her.

I wanted to spit in her face after she said that, but I stood up instead.

I wish I would help this bitch after telling me something like that.

I started to walk away but she followed me.

"Envy he loves you and you make him vulnerable. I've watched him ready to give up everything because of you, so I know that he loves you. Hell, he killed my sister, his own wife for you," Carmen said.

He what?

Carmen shook her head.

"He what?"

"There's so much more that we need to talk about. Just keep him busy. Occupied. Just until I have my baby and so I can get the hell out of town," Carmen said and walked off.

He did what?

If he killed her sister that meant that he killed his daughter too.

But why?

Why would Silas do something like that?

And because of me she'd said?

Huh?

I sat in the car and wondered if I could believe anything that Carmen had just told me.

I'll admit it, some of it made a whole lot of sense, but Carmen was evil at heart and believing her just didn't feel right.

But she'd even told me that she was behind me getting shot.

I was sure she wouldn't have said that she was behind it if she wasn't.

She hadn't had to tell me that but she had.

Maybe she was telling the truth.

Maybe she'd told me because she'd wanted me to somehow know how serious she was about everything that she was saying.

Even if she had to tell me a few secrets of her own.

But I had so many questions.

She'd said so many things, and there were so many things that I still wanted to know.

Oh, and Silas was such a liar!

Damn, he was the worst!

All of his half-ass truths made my ass itch, and now I was going right back into that space concerning him that I'd just come from.

He couldn't be trusted.

But Carmen had said that he loved me and if anyone knew how he really felt, than I was sure that it was her.

But why had he wanted to kill me?

When?

What was it about?

That part really had me wondering.

I'd never done anything to him but tell a few lies, but hell, he definitely couldn't have wanted to hurt me because of that.

Some of the things that I'd thought that I was lying to him about, he'd already known anyway, so I had no idea why he would have even thought about trying to kill me.

I just didn't know.

And then Carmen said that they'd put the whole hotel scheme together.

Wow.

Now that was just beyond crazy.

And clever as hell too.

I guess they'd wanted out as bad as they'd said that they did.

And they'd found the perfect way to do it.

But my question now was why would Silas want to kill Carmen?

Was it because he was jealous?

Was it because he felt betrayed?

And why was he just mad at Carmen and not Wiley too?

Carmen had mentioned that he had a few brothers and sisters, half ones anyway, yet he'd never mentioned that either.

Why?

As I drove down the road, my stomach started to cramp so I tried to stop stressing and thinking about all of the things that Carmen had told me.

But she had mentioned that there was more.

So I had to keep her alive so that I could find out.

That's if I could.

****

Chapter EIGHT

Everywhere Silas went, I went.

Every phone call he took, I was right there.

Why I was doing this for Carmen?

I wasn't sure.

I still didn't like her, not one bit.

But I mean, she was pregnant and all.

And though her parenting skills were up for question, the baby still needed a mother or at least to be safe while she was carrying him.

We hadn't spoken since that day, but she'd dropped more than enough bombs on me, and considering that she said that she had more, I wasn't sure that I was ready for them.

But I wanted to know what they were.

She'd said that Silas had wanted to kill me.

I didn't know when or why, but that was one of the main things that I was hoping to get out of her.

She'd also said that he'd killed her sister, which was also his deceased wife, for me.

How?

Why?

That just couldn't be true.

His wife and daughter had been hit by a drunk driver and the driver had died as well.

Silas damn sure was alive and living so I guess that would have meant that he would have had to order the hit.

But why would he do that?

And especially to his daughter?

No, he adored his daughter.

Hell, he loved my daughter more than words could explain, so Carmen just had to be wrong.

Something just wasn't right.

Something had been left out.

And Detective Wiley had shot me?

And Carmen had told him to?

Oh, I hadn't forgotten about that and I was going to make sure that both of them paid for what they'd done to me.

I wished that I could have told Silas, but since I had to find out some things on him from Carmen, and because Detective Wiley was his brother, it was probably better to keep my recent discoveries to myself.

But they all were going to get what was coming to him.

Sooner or later.

With Silas and Horizon napping on the other couch, I reached for my phone.

I was desperately awaiting my delivery date, but I still had a little while to go.

I was due two days before Valentine's Day and that was just too far away.

I went to search the fatal accident that involved Silas's previous wife and his daughter.

The story confirmed that the driver was drunk and it was a head on collision. Silas's wife, daughter, and the male driver were pronounced dead at the scene.

I looked at the pictures from the scene.

The photos of the wife and daughter matched the ones that I'd seen on Silas's obituary.

The man looked somewhat familiar, but I couldn't put his face to the name.

I glanced at Silas as he slept and wondered if he really had something to do with it all.

Horizon was resting comfortably in his arms.

It was truly a picture perfect moment and there was nothing that Carmen could have said to me that would make me believe that Silas would have killed his own daughter.

There was just no way.

His wife, for whatever reason, maybe I could believe that, but never would I believe that he killed his daughter.

She would have to come better than that.

But I couldn't put much of anything, past anyone, these days.

If you ask me, all of them had some major issues and they all were fighting harder than ever to make sure that their truths and secrets stayed hidden.

I was just caught up in the middle of it all and I hated it. I hated the soap opera that my life had become. I see why I had spent years by myself, in my own space and in my own little world.

People in this world were lunatics.

But little by little, I was getting fed up and when a woman is fed up, she gets up and does something about it.

I cyed Silas's phone and thought to go through it but I figured that he probably wasn't as asleep as he appeared to be.

He was always watching me these days and I was definitely watching him too.

I'll admit, I was definitely in my feelings about it all. I mean I just thought, for once, things were going to be okay.

Sure, someone was out to kill me, I think, but I was getting use to things with Silas going as well as they had been.

I was hoping that we were finally going to be drama free and that everything concerning him, was either out in the open, more or less, or pretty much done and over with.

But from the looks of it, I was never going to know all that there was to know about Silas.

And I wasn't sure if I was going to be able to live with it or not.

Still entertaining my thoughts, out of nowhere, my phone chimed and Carmen's name appeared.

It was a text message.

What was she up to now?

I was going to erase the message without bothering to actually read it and just mind my own business, but for the life of me, I just couldn't ignore it.

No matter how bad I'd wanted to, I just had to see what it was that she had to say.

I opened it to find that she'd asked me to meet her and she'd sent an address.

Should I go?

No, Carmen couldn't be trusted.

But maybe she had something else to say.

Something that I needed to hear.

Maybe I could find out some other truths about my husband that I was sure that he was never going to tell me.

I couldn't make up my mind for a while and after ten minutes, I gave in.

I was going to go and see what it was that Carmen wanted, and I hoped and prayed that I wouldn't regret it.

I tip-toed my big ass around the condo and headed out the door trying not to wake my family.

Silas hadn't popped up or hadn't called me as I pulled out of the parking lot, so he must have really been asleep.

I drove in a hurry.

I wasn't sure if was a good idea, but I was going anyway.

I hated Carmen.

And Carmen hated me.

I didn't care if she was trying to hide it or if she was only trying to act with some sense because she felt as though I could be some assistance to her, but I knew the truth.

And the truth was that we hated each other.

She still had some kind of twisted love for and loyalty to Silas, so at the end of the day, she was still my enemy.

And I had to remember to treat her as such.

Matter of a fact, it would be a good idea to go by the house and get my gun, to keep it in my purse.

Just in case.

Just to be safe.

These people were cold-hearted and they were sneaky.

And sneaky and cold-hearted just wasn't a good mix.

I pulled up at a house that wasn't exactly Carmen's taste.

It was old, and looked pretty much abandoned except for her car in the driveway.

As soon as I saw it, I decided that I wouldn't go inside, and I didn't have to because as soon as I placed the car in park, she came outside.

She wobbled to the car and got in.

"Whose house is this?" I asked Carmen.

"Oh, this is the house that I killed my family in. I bought it a few months ago from the owners."

What?

So she did do it?

So Silas had been telling the truth about her and her history?

Well, maybe he was on a roll with being honest and maybe Carmen was the one still lying.

I was surprised that Carmen had said the piece of information and hadn't tried to hide it like she had tried to before.

I guess she figured that since I was with Silas, there was no telling what he'd told me, or either it was that she just didn't give a damn anymore.

I could tell that she was tired.

But weren't we all?

"How could you be in the house that you killed your family in? And why aren't you at your other house?"

I was so uncomfortable that I started to drive, just in case something unexpected was about to happen.

This was a bad idea.

"They're dead already. Stop being so sensitive. And I can't go home. Silas knows where I live...duh. He wouldn't be caught dead on this side of town so I'm not worried about him finding me here. I need to know from you if he's said anything. As soon as the baby comes, I can make my move. I already have everything planned. I just can't take the baby with me. Has he said anything to you, about me?"

Carmen was shook!

I mean she was definitely afraid of something, or someone, and let her tell it, that someone was Silas.

Maybe she was just paranoid.

Or maybe she was right.

And if she was right, I had been wrong about the man that I'd decided to marry.

But Carmen's fright was real and it showed and as much as I wanted to enjoy it, I couldn't.

She was definitely acting out of character, and I for one knew how it felt to be scared for my life or concerned for my safety.

"No. He hasn't. Why don't you just fake your death? And cover it up the way you do everyone else's?"

"What the hell do you think I'm going to do? But I can't take this baby with me. I'm going to leave it with Wiley or somebody. Silas had been right all those years ago. I am not fit to be a mother. And doing it alone definitely wouldn't work. I don't love Wiley. He was a mistake. I tried to be friendly and see if there could possibly be anything but my heart will always belong to

Silas. Even though he's with you and even though I know he's trying to kill me. I'll probably never love again. If love is what you could call it. Can you find out what he's up to? I'll pay you or whatever you want me to do. You may need a favor one day; my kind of favors. You never know what you may need me to do."

Carmen was scaring me because she was so scared.

She wasn't all big and bad now, and truthfully, it was freaking me out.

I didn't need to be involved in this, especially being pregnant.

Whatever was going on, I didn't want to be or need to be a part of it.

I couldn't help her.

Hell if it was me, I was sure that she wouldn't help me. Hell she would have probably been trying to be the one pulling the trigger.

I'd been trying to stay on Silas, not necessarily for Carmen but for the baby.

But the thing is, I felt that if he really wanted Carmen, she would have really been dead a long time ago.

But then again, both of them had so many things on their side and in their back pockets, both of them were probably always two steps ahead of what the other one was thinking or trying to do.

We circled back around and pulled back up at the old, abandoned looking house.

This was the last time I was going to meet her, so I had to ask.

"Carmen why would Silas have wanted to kill me?"

She looked at me.

"Because you're her. You're her," Carmen said and got out of the car.

I'm her?

What did that mean?

Who was I?

What was Carmen talking about?

I drove back to the condo in silence with Carmen's words ringing in my ears.

Of course she knew something that I didn't know, but her loyalty to Silas kept the information that she told me limited.

That's a lot of damn loyalty to someone that she thought was trying to kill her.

I guess she figured that she had it all worked out if she could just disappear.

And she was planning to do it without the baby?

I guess she knew herself better than anyone else did. But I had to wonder if she really knew Silas just as well. Whether she did or she didn't, I needed to find out the truth behind her words.

She'd said them, and I knew that she'd meant them.

***

"Is there something you're not telling me?" Silas asked.

I looked at him innocently.

I had been trying my best to act normal, but it was hard with all of the things that Carmen had said, constantly in my head.

I hadn't talked to her since that night and she hadn't attempted to reach out to me.

I'd actually driven by the abandoned looking house, but her car wasn't there.

Maybe she was gone.

Whether she was gone by choice or by force, so to speak, I wasn't sure.

She had to be about due for delivery because I was and I wondered if she'd had the baby already and taken off, and if she had I wondered where the baby was.

Of course it crossed my mind as to whether or not Silas had done something to her.

But of course I couldn't ask him.

Not directly anyway.

"I'm fine. Have you heard from Carmen?" I asked.

"No. But to be straight up with you, I called her. A few times. When I saw that she was pregnant, I immediately became worried about that child. Carmen is not well. She can't be a mother to that baby. But she didn't answer or return my calls. So I didn't sweat it. It's past time for us to cut all ties. All of our *business* is handled. So the way I see it, it's good luck to her and good riddance. But I'm worried about you. My beautiful, amazing wife. You've put your store process on hold. You don't seem half as excited about it as you were before. So, what's wrong? Is it the baby hormones?"

I could tell that Silas was concerned.

It seemed so genuine, but Carmen had me second guessing him, again.

I just wanted to blurt everything out but I had seen his not-so friendly side and reactions when I said things that were out of line, and I didn't want to get on his bad side.

But I just wanted to know.

I needed to know why he initially had a problem with me. I needed to know why he'd wanted to kill me.

I needed to know if he'd really been behind his wife's death. And I definitely needed to know how was I this "her" as Carmen had mentioned.

But for now, I was just going to say nothing.

Knowing Carmen, all of this could be a load of bull crap.

She could have been lying about most of the things that she'd said, and maybe trying to mess things up between Silas and I, or for some other reason unknown.

You just never know these days.

"I'm okay. Just ready for the baby to come. I'm tired of being pregnant," I said to him.

He took my word for it, and went on about his business.

He was setting up the baby's crib in one of the spare bedrooms of the condo.

Since the driver of the Charger had yet to be found, we'd decided that we weren't going back to our perfect house.

Eventually we were going to have to get all of our things out of it and sell it, but we had too many other things to worry about at the time.

Of course we were going to have to find another house, but with the baby coming, for now, I liked the security of the condo. I liked the fact that we were in a building, around other people, so I did feel just a little bit safer in a way.

Hell, the danger was probably in my own home.

The knock at the door startled me and I headed to see who it was.

The only person that knew we were in the condo was Josephine, and she'd moved away, so I wondered who it was.

I peeked through the hole on the door and I was surprised to find that it was Detective Wiley.

But then again, in actuality, he was Silas's brother, so of course Silas probably told him where we were a long time ago.

But he would never admit to it.

And then again, maybe he had some news on who had killed Sonni and tried to kill me.

"Envy, I need to ask you a few questions."

Detective Wiley had his cop, asshole voice on, so I guess he was in character or maybe he was doing real police business.

Silas came into the living room.

I watched his expression.

It didn't break.

You would never even guess that they were brothers. They looked nothing alike and the way that Silas looked at him was as though he didn't know him at all.

Maybe Carmen really was up to no good.

But then again, Silas and Grant had pulled the same stunt, so he was probably just pretending.

"Carmen has been missing for a while now. You and she were spotted together at a children's department store a while back, and she hasn't been seen since. Have you heard from her? Do you know where she is?"

Silas looked at me as though he wanted to ask me when I'd seen her again.

Wiley had some nerve talking to me as though I didn't know about what was going on between him and Carmen.

So, he hadn't seen her?

Really?

Or was this a part of another one of their schemes?

Could be.

Maybe they were trying to fool Silas.

Wiley looked at me as though he didn't believe me.

"Where is she Envy?" Detective Wiley said in a tone that shocked me.

Oh, this he was serious.

It was as though he'd said forget all of the bull crap...he wanted answers!

"I don't know."

"Yes you do. Tell me."

He seemed to be getting upset.

Wow. He must really not know where Carmen is.

Oh hell, Carmen, what are you up to now?

"She said that she doesn't know."

"Silas, she's lying," Wiley said.

He called Silas by name.

Oh hell yeah, that was my opening to dig in.

"Oh so you two know each other?" I looked at them both.

"Leave her alone," Silas said to Wiley.

Wiley stood to his feet.

"How do you know each other?"

"Tell your wife who I am...brother," Wiley said.

So, Carmen was telling the truth!

At least about that.

They were indeed half-brothers.

Silas didn't look at all bothered by his statement.

It was almost as though he didn't care about the truth being exposed.

"Well if she doesn't know where she is, that leaves you. What did you do to her Silas?"

Uh oh.

"Nothing. I haven't seen her."

"Bullshit! Did you kill her? If so, then where is the baby?"

The way that he said the comments were almost as though he didn't really care all that much about Carmen. He was more concerned about the baby.

Looking at Silas's face, immediately I knew in my heart that Carmen had been wrong.

Silas hadn't killed her and I was sure that he didn't even want to.

"I don't know where she is," Silas said.

Call me silly, but Silas was just a little hurt that his brother was the father of Carmen's child.

I could see that he felt the same pain in a sense that Carmen had felt when he'd done it to her.

He was more hurt than angry.

More betrayed than revengeful.

I didn't know him as well as Carmen did, but I was sure that he truly hadn't seen her or done anything to her or the child.

My gut just had to be right on this one.

Wiley stared at Silas for another second or two, and without another word, he left.

It wasn't until the door shut behind him that I was actually able to breathe.

Silas sat beside me, knowing that yet again, he had some explaining to do.

"I didn't do anything to her, I swear. I really don't know where she is."

I rubbed my belly and continued to focus on my breathing.

I believed him.

I really did believe him.

But now was the time to see what I could get out of him.

And I wouldn't accept anything less than the truth.

"Carmen told me about the scheme to close the hotel and bring down the thirteenth floor. Was she telling truth? Was it all a scheme?"

Silas looked at me.

"Yes. So you have seen her?"

Tell him or don't tell him.

Aw hell, she was gone now more than likely anyway.

"Yes. And Detective Wiley is you brother? You guys have the same father?" I asked.

"Yes."

"Why hide the truth from me? Why not tell me about the hotel or about Wiley? Why?"

"You didn't need to know what was going down with the hotel. That was between us and something that we all had to do for ourselves. No one was supposed to ever know about that and I can't believe that Carmen even mentioned that to you. What was she thinking? Eventually I was going to tell you about my siblings, but I hadn't exactly figured out how. And things between Wiley and I had been tensed."

"Because he was seeing Carmen?"

"Yes. I didn't think that it would bother me. But it did. I don't want her, but he wasn't supposed to want her either.

But karma is a bitch ain't it? It is what it is. I had no right to feel any kind of way about their relationship. But I didn't kill her or do anything to her. If she's gone, she left on her own."

I felt some kind of way that Silas was a little jealous of their relationship.

But then again, he'd got just what he'd deserved.

He'd done the same thing to Carmen, and I was sure that in a way it was her payback.

That's what his ass gets!

"Well since we are being open, I have something to ask you. Something that Carmen also told me. Did you kill your wife and daughter? Carmen said that you did."

"No." Silas answered so fast that I knew that he found the question offensive.

I could see that he was trying not to get upset and that he didn't want to make the question more than it was.

Maybe he didn't hurt them.

That damn Carmen had me and my mind all messed up!

I just didn't know who to believe anymore.

But at this point, I was past tired of all of the drama and I was coming up with a plan of my own.

It didn't matter whether Silas was telling the truth or not.

I was up to something…

***

"Push! Push!" Silas screamed and soon after, I heard the cries of my precious baby boy.

Silas loved on him for a little and then reached him to me.

I kissed him immediately and smiled at how beautiful he was. He was so adorable and he was almost identical to Silas.

He was perfect.

That moment was perfect.

My family was complete.

Well, at least for the time being.

Though I loved Silas and I'd chosen to move forward with him by marrying him and giving him a baby, I was starting to think that it was all one big mistake.

I thought that all of the secrets had come out a long time ago, but things were still happening and don't nobody got time for that.

I had to get out.

I had to get away from it all but now that a child was involved I knew that it wasn't going to be easy.

Silas just wasn't going to let me just leave.

I was going to have to put up a fight.

He hadn't wanted me to leave before the marriage or before the child, so he surely wasn't going to let me just walk away from him now.

I could bet my life on it.

Still no one had heard from or seen Carmen.

She hadn't tried to reach out to me and I hadn't tried to reach out to her. I was sure that wherever she was, she had already had the baby and she was probably far, far away.

She was probably someone under a different name and look by now, and I wondered if the baby was safe.

I knew that Wiley didn't have it, so I wondered who did.

In my opinion, just thinking of Wiley's responses and the way that he'd acted when he'd showed up at our condo that day, I think that Carmen had it all confused.

I don't think that it was Silas that had been trying to kill her.

I had a feeling that it was Wiley.

For what reason, who knows, but I just didn't think that it was Silas.

But still yet, Silas had to go.

He just had to.

Our stay at the hospital was memorable and I tried to cherish each moment with him, since I knew that it was all going to have to come to an end.

Some way or another, I was getting out.

My mind was made up.

If I didn't, I felt that I would spend the rest of my life looking over my shoulder.

I would spend the rest of my life fearing what could happen or wondering what else Silas had in his bag full of bones that could possibly come out and hurt us.

And no one could live like that.

At least they couldn't live like that and truly be happy.

And I just wanted to be happy.

The suggestion that Silas had mentioned a while ago often crossed my mind.

If we ran away together, started brand new, in a place where no one knew who we were, maybe things would be better.

Maybe things of the past would be easier to forget.

Maybe I could be happy with him then.

Maybe.

But I just couldn't be sure. The only thing that I was sure about was that I now had two children and they needed me. They needed me healthy. They needed me sane. And they needed me happy so that I could be the best mother that I could possibly be to them.

Our first night back at the condo, I watched the baby sleep for hours.

It was almost as though I couldn't believe that he was mine.

He was just so precious.

I'd always wanted mama to give me a baby brother but that never seemed to happen.

Daddy wanted another baby, but Mama was so busy trying to be super woman that what he wanted after a while didn't exactly matter.

But that hadn't stopped him from trying to teach us everything there was to know about football and other things that we could have cared less about.

But a son, a son would have really made him happy.

And now I had one and he was truly a blessing.

I just wanted him to be safe. I just wanted both of my babies and myself to be safe.

And the cold reality was that being with Silas, just wasn't safe.

It never had been.

And it never would be.

I knew that if I was going to make a move, I was going to have to do it soon.

And I knew just who I was going to get to help me.

****

Chapter NINE

I was definitely dealing with postpartum depression.

I was down and out and I couldn't do anything for my kids, Silas, or even myself.

Considering the other things that were heavy on my mind and heart, I was sure that it had made it all a lot worse.

I was damn near suicidal.

Every day I seemed to cry more and more and the more I cried, the more detached from my family and the world I became.

I hadn't held my son in over a week and Horizon was stuck with Silas doing her hair every morning and getting her dressed for school.

My poor baby looked a hot as mess most of the time, but I couldn't seem to make myself do a thing about it.

I just couldn't shake the feeling of anxiety and worry and I just couldn't pull myself together.

"I fixed you some food baby," Silas said.

He sat the food in front of me and then sat right beside me.

"I'm not moving until you eat," Silas said.

Of course he was being the good husband, but I didn't trust him or his actions half of the time.

What I felt for him was no longer love.

I really didn't know what it was.

"Baby I want you to get better. We love you. And besides, I don't have any titties for little man to lie on, and I think he's starting to notice," Silas said.

Surprisingly, I smiled.

I didn't want to, but I did.

Why did he have to be all of the bad things and not enough of the good?

At one point I thought that the good outweighed the bad, but with all of the new bull crap and discoveries; I was surely wrong.

So now I have to make my wrong choice, a right one.

And the right thing, the best thing for me to do was leave him.

"I love you so much. I can't imagine my life without you. You're my baby, my lady, my wifey, and my friend. Now please get better and come back to me. Daddy misses you. And *he* do too," Silas winked and I smiled again.

He didn't keep his word by sticking around to make me eat, and soon he exited the room.

I placed the food on the table and crawled back under the covers.

Damn…I was really going to miss him.

***

"Envy slow down," Wiley said as I tried to rush to my Escalade.

The Toyota was gone, and I had only driven the Porsche from last year's Valentine's Day once.

He'd made it to the door just as I was closing it, and held it open with his hand.

For the past few weeks I had been doing a lot better and slowly but surely I was getting back to myself.

The postpartum was definitely going away.

I had just come out of the grocery store from getting the baby's formula and Detective Wiley had been waiting for me to come out.

"Envy, I just wanted to talk to you."

I didn't have anything to say to him.

Not only was he a part of tricking me with the whole hotel thing, he had also shot me for Carmen and hid the fact that he was Silas's brother.

He was so amped about finding some damn head honchos, when he shared the same blood with one of them the whole time.

People were a damn trip!

And he too was going to pay for shooting me.

I was going to make sure that my justice was served.

"We don't have anything to talk about. And if you bother me again, don't think that I won't go to the station and tell them about you little *extra-curricular* activities. Dirty cops are the worst and I'm sure they would have a field day making you pay for all of the crimes you have committed. What would happen if they knew about your involvement in the hotel case or that you were the finger on the trigger that shot me? Oh, did you think that I didn't know that it was you? Carmen told me."

"Envy look. I'm just looking for Carmen and my son. Did she tell you anything about where she might go? Or what she might do? I've done enough dirt. I just want my son. She has my son, wherever she is, and I just want to at least get the chance to be his father."

I didn't feel a bit of sympathy for him.

Screw him and his pity party.

"I have to go," I said to him and he let go of the car door.

He hit the alarm on the car that was parked right beside mine.

I glared at him and then back at the car.

I rubbed my eyes to make sure that I was seeing things right.

He wasn't driving his police car, or the jeep that I'd seen him in a few times.

It was the red Charger with the tinted windows; the one that had hit and killed Sonni, and the one that had tried to hit me.

He'd wanted me to see it.

He'd wanted me to know.

I grabbed my phone, and rolled down my window as he stood there as though he was waiting on me to ask him.

"Why?"

He looked at me as though he had changed his mind about saying anything.

At this point, knowing wouldn't change anything and I knew that somehow he would get out of it even if I'd tried to report him.

But that wasn't going to stop me from trying.

"Was it Carmen who put you up to it huh? Why?"

"It wasn't Carmen's idea. Not the second time. Your sister's death was ordered by Silas, which I'm sure you already know why. And yours was ordered by…your sister Josephine."

What?

I just didn't understand.

Josephine wanted me dead?

But why?

He's lying!

"She hated and loved you all at the same time. You didn't know this, but Grant sort of had a thing for you. She'd said it was more of the idea of you, or at least what he'd fabricated you to be in his mine. He always compared her to you. He wanted her to look like you and dress like you. He even wanted her to act like you. Whether it was because he wanted you and couldn't have you, or if it was just infatuation, or because he damn worshiped Silas and his choices and taste in everything, he wanted her to do everything just like you. From how she explained it to me, her breaking point was while she was cleaning Grant one day, he called out your name. He hadn't said any other word, but he managed to say Envy. The doctor's said he would never speak, yet he spoke your name. I would have probably beaten the life out of him, right then and there but that was the last straw for her. She'd planned on killing him too but Silas stepped in. But she still wanted your head. She wanted you gone. Of course Grant had her in the loop a little more than you think, and she reached out to me. She knew enough about me. Enough for me to take the job. She offered me a few of Grant's millions to get the job done. It wasn't personal. It was just business. But I missed. I never miss, unless it was on purpose, like the first time. But I missed. She saw it as a sign. Called it off. Paid me for trying and moved away. Of course Silas and I went to war over it, since you'd managed to get a glimpse of the car. Silas wanted answers, but I denied it. And I put the blame on Carmen. I told him about our relationship and said that she must have taken the car while I was asleep. This car was supplied to me personally by him, for dirty work, so I had to put it on someone with access to it."

Scandalous!

Loyalty was nowhere in his back pocket.

Apparently he didn't care about anyone, accept getting what he wanted out of the deal.

He was just like everyone else.

But I was still devastated over what he'd just told me and revealed to me about Josephine.

I had no idea she felt that way about me!

I loved her so much and she'd tried to have me killed?

My feelings were so hurt.

And Grant wanted her to be me?

He actually wanted her to be like me?

Hell, for years, I didn't even want to be me.

I didn't have anything. I was nothing to admire or to put on a pedestal, and I couldn't believe that he thought that Josephine wasn't good enough.

He'd always seemed to love her so much.

He'd taken a bullet for her and almost died trying to save her.

He'd given up his entire life so that she could have hers.

It just didn't make sense.

But I knew that it was the truth.

I just knew that it was the truth.

And for that alone, I was so angry!

Grant had driven my sister to despise me enough to try and have me killed because he wanted her to be me, for some stupid ass reason.

I hoped he croaked over and died.

I really did.

"Don't hold it against her. She knows it was wrong. At the time, she was angry and in a bad place. And of course, Silas knew Sonni was back in town and up to no good. She had some dirt on him and she'd actually come to the police station and guess who she spoke to. Me. She gave me a few copies of pictures and recordings not knowing that Silas was my brother. I told him and he told me to take care of her. I followed her to your house that day. I didn't expect you to be outside. Silas said that he was picking you up and you were supposed to be gone. You weren't supposed to be there. You weren't supposed to see it."

I just had no words.

The car was running.

And…my phone was still recording.

I said nothing because there was nothing for me to say.

But now I knew, more than ever that I had to get away from it all and I had to do it fast.

I was done.

I was done with Silas.

I was done with everything.

I was done!

"And Carmen. Well, I wasn't exactly trying to kill her. I just wanted to scare her and have a little fun with her. She was carrying my baby, I wouldn't have killed her. At least not while she was pregnant. But that little bitch managed to get away. And I can't find her. Nevertheless, everything that I have ever done, was all for money. I was raised by a single mother and I've had to work hard for everything that I have. And never seemed to have enough. But now, I'm set for life."

Still not responding, I put the car in reverse, but suddenly I thought of a question.

It was still the one thing that I didn't know.

"Do you know what it is that Silas has against me? Well, maybe not now, but in the beginning? Why did he initially want to kill me?"

Wiley opened his car door.

"Now that is something that you are going to have to ask him. Seems like you to have a lot to talk about. By the way, did he ever tell you how he met Carmen?"

"Um, he ran into her one day, and thought that she was her sister at first or something like that. Carmen had just gotten out of the mental institution."

"Or maybe he met her in there. Hey Envy, do me a favor. Tell my brother goodbye for me," Wiley said, got into the car and drove away.

I was stumped.

I mean I was just...

I didn't even know what to say that I was.

What was Wiley trying to say?

So the way that Silas and Carmen met was a lie?

Oh my, this was all just too much!

My head was spinning as I started to drive away.

Why was everything in my life so messed up?

What was I going to do?

Something had to be done.

Something just had to give.

After what I'd just heard, I couldn't trust anyone and I had to do something.

My life obviously depended on it and so did my babies.

There was no way in hell that I could be in this mess any longer than I had to be.

These people had destroyed my life.

They destroyed my family.

And Silas was just as guilty as everyone else.

Pulling up at home, my mind started to work out all of the specifics.

I decided that my original plot to get away from Silas and this life, just wasn't going to work.

But what I had in mind this time just might do it.

I found my phone and made a phone call.

Surprisingly, it ranged on the other end and I knew that there was no turning back.

***

"Can I taste you?"

I looked at Silas with the side eye.

My first thought was hell no, but since it was about to go down, I might as well enjoy the pleasures of his tongue one last time.

As Silas licked and kissed on my *lips*, I toggled my thoughts between what he was doing to me, and what he'd done to me.

He was truly a devil in disguise and I had to get away from him and everything and everybody surrounding or involving him.

I just had to.

I forced myself to concentrate on his tongue and it didn't take long for all of the empty spaces of the room to become filled with my moans of satisfaction.

Soon my legs started to shake and my eyes rolled into the back of my head.

It was time for me to release my *frustrations* inside of his mouth, one last time.

As he smacked his lips, I waited for him to move because I knew that he was going to want me to return the favor.

How do you give a blow job to your husband knowing that you no longer wanted to be with him?

In a way, I felt like I was servicing one of my old clients.

I was just doing it because I kind of had to and not because I wanted to.

Swallowing his *rod*, it didn't take Silas long to get into it and I worked overtime to get him to where he needed to be so that it could all be over.

Silas moaned and told me he loved me but I no longer cared whether he did or not.

I was done.

Once he reached his point of no return, I allowed him to release himself, I swallowed it, and then I headed to the bathroom.

I felt disgusted.

At that moment, I knew that I was absolutely, positively, done with our relationship.

Our marriage was over.

I came back into the bedroom to see Silas sitting on the edge of the bed.

He was smiling.

He looked relaxed.

But I was about to rock his world…and not in the way that he probably wanted me to.

It was now or never.

I headed to my purse, picked it up and stood in front of him.

I'd gone by our house the day before to get the pictures that had been in the box that Sonni had left on the front porch over a year ago.

Getting the pictures out of my purse, I threw them at him.

Silas looked at them and then looked at me.

"So, who is the man in the pictures Silas?"

"Where did you get these?"

"That's not what I asked you. Who is he?"

Silas sighed.

"I'm sure you already know."

He was right.

I did.

After I'd thought about it long and hard, I put two and two together and remembered where I'd saw the man from the accident with Silas's deceased wife and daughter.

I'd seen him on the pictures that were in the box.

He was the man in the pictures talking to Silas and where he'd appeared to be having a meeting with him or something.

"So, you paid him to kill your wife and daughter? You paid him to kill them?"

"No. I paid him to kill my wife. My daughter was never supposed to be in the car. She'd picked her up from school early that day without telling me. She wasn't supposed to be with her."

Silas shook his head in regret.

"Why?"

"Because she wouldn't leave. I'd asked her for a divorce, and she wouldn't leave. But I needed her to leave so that I could have my opportunity with you. And as for him, he was terminally ill and dying anyway. He owed me."

What did he mean his *opportunity* with me?

"As much power as you had or still have, you had options. You didn't have to kill her."

"Yes I did. She would have ruined everything."

Silas sounded insane.

"But I thought she was the love of your life."

"She was. But something else was more important at the time."

"Me?"

"Yes."

"Why Silas? What about me?"

"It's complicated."

Like hell it was.

"Silas, where did you really meet Carmen?"

"I told you."

"You told me a lie. I'm asking you to tell me the truth."

Detective Wiley's comment told me that it was more to the story of how Carmen and Silas met and I had a feeling that it would make what I was about to do even easier.

Silas was uncomfortable.

But I wasn't letting up.

"Tell me."

"Okay Envy. My childhood was horrible. I was beat, tortured, all because I was the product of mother's affair. Her husband, my step-father hated me. Every chance that he could, he did something to hurt me or degrade me. He made me pay for my mother's transgression over and over again. Do you know what it's like to be young and not understanding why things, horrible things were always happening to you?"

I looked at Silas as I watched him hold back tears and fight emotions that were desperately trying to get the best of him.

"When it was time for me to come here, I couldn't wait, and pretty much cut all ties, except when it involved business. I even kept a distance from my mother just because she was tied to everything that I was trying to forget. I really did meet Nicole, Carmen's sister, at the bank, but things didn't go exactly like I'd told you. We actually dated and became an item. But there's something that I didn't tell you. I have a disorder. I have the same thing that Sonni had. Multiple personality disorder. I actually met her, Sonni, for the first time in person, outside of my therapist's office at the time. She knew she needed help, but she wouldn't go in. She couldn't accept it. She couldn't accept the fact that she was sick. She just stood there and wouldn't make that step to go in and get what she needed. I offered her lunch and after only an hour around her, I knew exactly what she was suffering from. But she wouldn't take my advice and get help. But she told me that she was having money problems. And I was the one that referred her to Carmen and the hotel. I'm off topic, but going back, I'm okay as long as I take my medicine, but sometimes I get so busy that I forget, sometimes things can get ugly. So, while dating Carmen's sister, Nicole, I had been running around and had gone almost a week without them and ended up beating a man near death," Silas took a second to catch his breath.

I was holding mine.

"Of course I had therapy records, medication and a diagnosis trail here in the states of what was wrong with me but the judge ordered me to serve a few months in the mental hospital anyway…which is where I actually met Carmen. My illness had come from my childhood I was sure. And the only one that had ever understood me was myself. And Grant. Grant was always there to help me. But then I met Carmen. She was so crazy, but as I said she was so smart and brilliant at the same time. I just can't quite explain it. But somewhere in the midst of it all, we became close. Of course she reminded me of Nicole, because they do look alike, but I didn't think anything of it. But when it was time for me to go, I promised her that I would pull every string that I could to get her out, and give her a job, and that's exactly what I did. She was supposed to rot in there but I got her out of there. That's why I say that she owed me her life. Once I was out and back in control of my life and everything else, I continued to see Nicole, and started seeing Carmen too. It was as though one side of me loved Nicole and the other side of me loved Carmen. I was literally two different men it seemed and I was always torn in between the two. Somehow, after a while, the side that loved Carmen, won. Spare of the moment, something came over me and I married Carmen. And just my luck, the same day that we tied the night, Nicole knocked on the door and Carmen answered. It was the first time in years that the sisters had come face to face. They knew who each other were, though Carmen really had lied at the time and told me that her whole family was dead. Nicole said she'd never mentioned her because she'd only met her a few times and all she knew was that she was sick and her adopted parents didn't allow her to see her as much as she would have wanted to."

What a big, hot mess!

But I was eager for Silas to finish the story.

"I had to choose, and since I'd eloped with Carmen, I chose her at the time. But the other man in me, the more logical, highly medicated, rational man, over time, disagreed with my decision. It seemed as though I had a better chance at being just a normal regular man, without Carmen. Carmen just seemed to get worse while out in the real world. She just had so many issues. So, eventually, I divorced her. Gave her plenty of money and I allowed her to stay at the hotel pretty much so that I could keep an eye on her. I felt responsible for her. That's the real reason I kept her around for so long, other than the fact that she handled business like a boss. Strangely, I still felt something for Nicole and after a while she took me back. We got married and everything else you pretty much know," Silas said.

I consumed everything that he'd said and I'd come to one conclusion.

Silas and Carmen deserved each other.

They really did.

They were both certified lunatics and a danger to society and they deserved to be locked away and someone needed to throw away the key.

I'd seen a few different sides of Silas, but never did I think it was anything to this extent.

"I know everything except why you killed her...your wife."

"I killed her because..."

I waited.

And I waited.

"I killed her because she found out that I was going to kill you," Silas said.

And there it is.

There was the truth.

But why?

"I really did try to divorce her so that I could pursue you, but she said no. She wouldn't leave or sign the damn papers. And going through my phone one night, she discovered that I was up to something. She saw emails of information that I had on you and other things that she'd had no business seeing. She'd even tried to attempt to hold it over my head as some kind of leverage to keep me in the marriage. So it was easier just to kill her. But I never meant to hurt my daughter I swear. I have to live with that every day and if I could take it back I would. I would have let Nicole lived and found another way to deal with her had I known that my daughter was going to die too," Silas said.

I held on to my purse tightly, and though he motioned for me to take a seat beside him, I stayed as far away from him as I could.

"I've known who you were for a long time, even when you were with Keymar. I even knew that Sonni your sister when I met her. I'd recognized her. I'd done my research. But my problem was with you. It was only with you. I was going to hurt you a few times, especially once Keymar was gone, but you had Horizon. I always found some kind of sympathy for you. I was always watching you, more or less. Rodney and his wife, the next door neighbors, they worked for me. I hadn't killed them, but I was going to because they'd crossed the line and caused a problem. They'd had a job to do and nothing else. But as I said, they worked for me. And the neighbors that lived there before them, and after them, worked for me. Even the neighbors at the new house worked for me too. I needed eyes on you at all times. Even when I wasn't around."

So I was officially scared to death!

I was scared for my life, and I had a feeling that Silas knew it too.

"I watched you all the time at the hotel, especially on surveillance footage. Even when you were downstairs. I didn't know what I wanted to do with you. I just knew that I wanted you to suffer. I just didn't know how. I was always somewhere watching you or following you. Every job application you done, I made sure to do what I had to do to make sure that you weren't hired. I wanted your only option to be the hotel, so that I could see you. Sonni actually overheard Carmen and I having a conversation about you and killing my wife one day, which is what she'd somehow managed to record and she'd hired someone to follow me and take the pictures. That's what the blackmail was about. And once she saw that we were an item, she threatened to expose me. I tried to keep her living because of my love for you, but she was working my last damn nerve. I just had to get rid of her."

I wanted to say so much yet I knew that it was in my best interest if I said nothing at all.

All that he'd said had me shook but he still hadn't told me the meat of it all.

Why me?

What did I ever do to him?

"With Nicole gone, I was free to get close to you. I was going to make you fall in love with me and then torture you or beat you, or something, but that required too much energy. Then I was just going to get in close enough, marry you, adopt Horizon, then kill you and have my daughter back in a sense, but something changed. As I got to know you, I fell for you. I didn't want to love you, but I did. Every day that I saw you. Every time that I touched you. I loved you even more. You became my weakness," Silas said.

It was weird that he'd used the same words as Carmen had to describe what I was to him.

But none of it made sense.

I still didn't understand.

"Silas, what did I do to you?"

He looked at me.

"You took my Daddy from me."

What?

What the hell was he talking about?

"The man that you called "Uncle Johnnie" was my real father. He was the love of my mother's life. But you lied on him and sent him to prison. You killed him."

What!

Okay, wait a minute.

Uncle Johnnie was the man that my grandparents had taken in when he was just a boy. He wasn't my real uncle, but his parents passed away so they finished raising him. He was the drunk that had a thing for my little sister Tia.

The one that I'd cried wolf on and had him sent to prison, where he'd fallen ill almost immediately and died.

He was Silas's dad?

He was the one that his mother had had an affair with?

We'd all known that Uncle Johnnie had a lot of kids, spread out everywhere, but Silas?

Silas was his son?

"As soon as I was here, I looked for him. I found out everything on him. Found all of his kids. Then I got one of my connections to get me all of the records from prison and from the trial and your testimonies. All I saw throughout all of the paperwork, over and over, was how many times he said that you lied. I could just tell as a man that he was telling the truth. He was innocent wasn't he?"

Was it a good idea to tell him the truth?

"I'm over it now. But I just have to know."

Oh well, this whole thing was about to be over anyway.

"Yes. He was actually trying to molest Tia. So, I cried wolf to keep him away from her. I didn't know that he was going to die. But I was trying to save my sister."

Silas didn't say anything for a while.

"Had he been alive, maybe he could have saved me. Maybe I could have come here with him and never went back. My mother hated the way her husband treated me. Maybe he would have wanted me. I waited for the day that I could get here and reunite with him and tell him all of the things that I had been through so that he could tell me, as my father, that he had my back now and that everything was going to be fine. But when I got here, I found out that he was dead. Dead because of you. So, yes, I hated you. I planned to make you pay for years. But once I finally got a hold of you, I didn't want to let you go. I started to forgive you. And I just wanted you. But people in my circle were constantly trying to mess it all up."

The more and more Silas talked, the easier it became for me to do what I had to do.

I was caught up in a nightmare and I was going to take my way out.

I felt bad for what he'd gone through and even a little disturbed that I had taken his father away from him in a way, but from all of the things that Silas had said, if I didn't do something about it now, no one ever would.

Silas stood up.

"But that's it. That's all of my secrets. There's nothing else to hide. I want you. I want my family. I want my kids. I want us," Silas said and started towards me.

Envy, if you are going to do this, you had better do this now. You can't trust him. You aren't safe with him. This is the only way.

My conscious was working overtime to convince me, and I had to go with my gut on this one.

Silas continued towards me, and before I could change my mind, I took the gun out of my purse and pointed it at him.

"Envy what are you doing?"

"I want out Silas. This is the only way," I said pointing the gun at him.

Silas looked at me as though I'd broken his heart in a million little pieces.

He looked at me as though he couldn't believe that I would even think about hurting him.

The question was, could I really do it?

Could I do it for me and my kids?

I'd thought that I could do it, but I couldn't.

But I knew if I tried to divorce him, he would probably kill me. He wasn't just going to let me walk away from him.

This was the only way.

"Envy. I love you," Silas said raising his hands.

Damn it!

I started to lower the gun and…

Boom.

Boom.

I looked over and saw Carmen standing in the bedroom.

Where the hell did she come from?

"I knew that you weren't going to be able to do it," she said, and waved the key at me.

"This was actually the condo that we lived in when we were married. I still had the spare," Carmen said.

I shook my head and looked back at Silas.

The blood was oozing from his head and painting the pearly white carpet a crimson, bloody red.

He was dead.

My husband was dead.

I'd called Carmen and found out that she was still alive.

I lied to her and told her that Silas was out to kill her and that he was doing everything in his power to find her.

I told her that I wanted out and since he was trying to kill her, and that being with him was killing me, I needed her help to do something about it.

Scared for her life, she agreed, and together, we came up with the plan to kill him and cover it up.

Who would have thought that Carmen and I would be partners in crime?

Surely not me I'll tell you that much.

But we were both desperate.

She was still in a paranoid state and she felt as though it was either him or her, though I knew that Wiley was the one that had been bothering her the whole time.

But everyone else was lying to get what they wanted and this was the only way.

Horizon started to call my name from her bedroom and I looked at Silas one last time.

He was gone.

I hadn't actually pulled the trigger as planned, but I felt as though I had.

I was supposed to shoot him and then call Carmen so she could do whatever it was that she done to cover things up.

But now she was going to be covering up her own murder, and in a way, my conscious was clear.

I glanced at Carmen who was obviously about to break down.

It was clear that in different ways, we both loved him.

And we both had to make a hard decision.

But we both also knew that it was the right one.

"Follow the plan Envy. Go to the other house. I'll start the cover up. No one will even know that he's dead for a while, if ever. I haven't decided yet. You'll still have all access to his money and a bulk of it was moved to a personal account already. The cards are with all of the other stuff. After tomorrow, leave, and don't ever look back. Don't come back here Envy. Silas doesn't talk to his family. His half siblings only knew of him, except for

Wiley, but according to what you said, he won't be looking for him either. He's probably gone too. No family. No friends. We just got away with the perfect crime. Now go. Goodbye Envy," Carmen said and with that, I got my babies, and I drove to the other house just like she'd said.

Since I didn't have to worry about Wiley coming after me, I wasn't scared to be in the house alone, but still I was up all night.

I couldn't believe what had taken place but I kept telling myself that this had been for the best.

Carmen had a buyer for the house, so the house would be sold, with Silas's fake signatures of course and now all I had to do was figure out where we were going.

She'd bought the Porsche from me herself, and the boat.

I'd called off all store building plans and everything had pretty much been taken care of.

I was just going to take off with Horizon and I would figure out the whole school thing along the way.

My only worry now was figuring out what was next.

One of Carmen's connections also gave me a brand new name, and a whole new life.

I had a fresh start.

To the world, Envy was now dead too.

I wanted to join Josephine and the other and pretend as though I didn't know what she'd done.

But the safest thing to do would be to never contact her again, and I figured that it was probably what was for the best.

I wasn't sure where I would end up.

All I knew was that I was free.

The morning came too fast and with the car already loaded up, the kids and I headed outside.

I stopped in my tracks as I stared at the baby in the car seat on the front porch, surrounded by black bags; my black bags full of cash.

The baby was asleep, so I sat down my carrier with my son in it and read the note attached to the other baby's car seat.

"Cleaning up a murder had to be worth more than just keeping tabs for me. The way I see it, you still owe me. He needs a mother. And not one like me. Oh and here's your money. Silas hid it at my house. Figured I would give it back."

This bitch here!

I called Carmen's phone…but it was disconnected.

I looked at the baby.

Oh what the hell.

He was probably safer with me anyway.

I got all three children situated in the car, put the money in the trunk and found an envelope on the passenger seat.

It was the baby's fake information.

She'd changed his name and everything to fit my new identity and the new identity that she'd given the kids.

People with money I tell you.

Ready to ride, I drove to the nearest gas station.

I had no idea where the road was going to take me or where the wind was going to blow me but I was ready.

I was ready.

Just before throwing my old phone in the trash can by the gas pumps just as Carmen had told me to, I sent Wiley a text message and told him where Carmen told me she was headed and the name that she was using.

I also smiled because I knew that I'd dropped the recording of all of his confessions at the grocery store that day off at the police station. I'd taken it from my phone and saved it to a disk.

So, if he wasn't out of town, yet, maybe they would get him. And if she wasn't already out of town, maybe he would get her.

Payback.

I started to hum as I pumped the gas but I was interrupted.

"Envy?"

I turned around to see that it was Gerald.

Gerald was the oil tycoon that used to *reserve my curves*, but stopped seeing me because he ran off and got married.

He was the one that had wanted me to run off with him.

"Hi. How are you? What have you been up too?"

"Well let's see. Married. Miserable. Divorced. Happy," Gerald said.

I smiled.

"And you?"

"Married. Kids, times three. Widowed." I answered.

Gerald looked into the back seat and smiled.

"They are beautiful. I know this might sound a little strange, but I never stopped thinking about you. I wished you would have just taken my offer and ran away with me," Gerald said.

Hmm…

Maybe it wasn't too late.

What was there to lose?

Hell, what's the worst that could happen?

Unless he was another Silas.

But I knew him, kind of, or at least I used to know him. I screwed him for months and talked about everything under the sun with him.

He told me his secrets and everything else.

I knew him enough.

"Ask me again."

Gerald looked at me.

He smiled.

"What?"

"Ask me again."

"Runaway with me. You. Me. And the kids. Anywhere. Everywhere."

I smiled.

"Yes."

We chatted for a second more and I agreed to follow him to his private jet, which was in the next city over.

He'd actually said that he'd came down for business and had just rode by the hotel on his way out.

He knew that it had been shut down, and he was one of the lucky ones whose name must have not been on any of the paperwork that I'd managed to grab and turn in.

He'd said that no one had ever came for him so he pretended as though it had never happened.

This was crazy!

This was insane!

But my gut told me that this was going to be the best decision that I'd ever made.

Gerald got into his car and pulled up beside mine.

"You ready for forever?"

"Is forever ready for me?"

"I was ready years ago. And this time, I won't ever let you go," he said.

I smiled.

"Oh, by the way, Envy wasn't my real name. My real name is...Tia."

What...I just liked the name.

It was Carmen's idea to use it.

And hell, by using it, in a way I felt that I was taking her with me wherever I go.

Gerald nodded and drove off as I followed.

As we entered the highway, I looked behind me in my rearview mirror.

I looked back at the tall, glass buildings.

I looked back at the city that had brought me more pain than it'd ever brought me joy.

I looked back at my past and knew that it would never be a part of my future.

I smiled as I left behind everything I'd ever known.

"See you later…or not," I said out loud and I never looked back again.

■■

The End

Review on Amazon:

http://www.amazon.com/s/ref=nb_sb_noss?url=search-alias%3Daps&field-keywords=bm%20hardin

Author B.M. Hardin's contact info:

Facebook: http://www.facbook.com/authorbm

Twitter: @BMHardin1

Instagram: @bm_hardin

Email:bmhardinbooks@gmail.com

www.ingramcontent.com/pod-product-compliance
Lightning Source LLC
Chambersburg PA
CBHW020617260626
47157CB00003B/1054